My dear mouse friends,

Have I ever told you how much I love science fiction? I've always wanted to write incredible adventures set in another dimension, but I've never believed that parallel universes exist . . . until now!

That's because my good friend Professor Paws von Volt, the brilliant, secretive scientist, has just made an incredible discovery. Thanks to some mousetropic calculations, he determined that there are many different dimensions in time and space, where anything could be possible.

The professor's work inspired me to write this science fiction adventure in which my family and I travel through space in search of new worlds. We're a fabumouse crew: the spacemice!

I hope you enjoy this intergalactic adventure!

Geronimo Stilton

PROFESSOR
PAWS VON VOLT

THE SPACEMICE

GERONIMO STILTONIX

TRAP STILTONIX

THEA STILTONIX

GRANDFATHER WILLIAM STILTONIX

ROBOTIX

BENJAMIN STILTONIX AND BUGSY WUGSY

Geronimo Stilton

RESCUE
REBELLION

Scholastic Inc.

Copyright © 2014 by Edizioni Piemme S.p.A., Palazzo Mondadori, Via Mondadori 1, 20090 Segrate, Italy.

International Rights © Atlantyca S.p.A.

English translation © 2015 by Atlantyca S.p.A.

The publisher does not have any control over and does not assume any responsibility for author or third-party websites or their content.

Based on an original idea by Elisabetta Dami.

www.geronimostilton.com

Published by Scholastic Inc., 557 Broadway, New York, NY 10012. SCHOLASTIC and associated logos are trademarks and/or registered trademarks of Scholastic Inc.

Stilton is the name of a famous English cheese. It is a registered trademark of the Stilton Cheese Makers' Association. For more information, go to www.stiltoncheese.com.

This book is a work of fiction. Names, characters, places, and incidents are either the product of the author's imagination or are used fictitiously, and any resemblance to actual persons, living or dead, business establishments, events, or locales is entirely coincidental.

ISBN 978-0-545-83538-1

Text by Geronimo Stilton
Original title *Il pianeta dei cosmosauri ribelli*
Cover by Flavio Ferron
Illustrations by Giuseppe Facciotto (design) and Daniele Verzini (color)
Graphics by Chiara Cebraro and Francesca Sirianni

Special thanks to AnnMarie Anderson
Translated by Lidia Morson Tramontozzi
Interior design by Kevin Callahan / BNGO Books

12 11 10 9 8 7 6 5 4 3 2 1   15 16 17 18 19 20/0

Printed in the U.S.A.   40
First printing 2015

In the darkness of the farthest galaxy in time and space is a spaceship inhabited exclusively by mice.

This fabumouse vessel is called the **MouseStar 1**, and I am its captain!

I am Geronimo Stiltonix, a somewhat accident-prone mouse who (to tell you the truth) would rather be writing novels than steering a spaceship.

But for now, my adventurous family and I are busy traveling around the universe on exciting intergalactic missions.

THIS IS THE LATEST ADVENTURE OF THE SPACEMICE!

DARKER THAN A BLACK HOLE!

It all started on a Friday. But it wasn't a regular Friday — it was a very **special** Friday. Every mouse in the galaxy had been **squeaking** about this Friday for days — no, weeks — no, months! That's because it was the release date for the *5-D* mega mouserific movie, *The Lord of the Asteroids*. And you know what it means to see a *5-D* mega mouserific movie, right? It means strapping yourself into the movie theater's floating seat to watch fabumouse **holograms*** and intergalactic visual

* A hologram is a three-dimensional image that is projected from a light source.

effects while listening to the universe's most superstellar surround-sound system!

Oh, excuse me! I forgot to introduce myself. My name is Stiltonix, Geronimo Stiltonix. I'm the captain of the legendary MOUSESTAR 1, the most mousetropic spaceship in the universe! Now, what was I squeaking about? Oh, right! I had promised my nephew Benjamin and his friend Bugsy Wugsy that I would take them to see *The Lord of the Asteroids* that Friday.

"Uncle, we're ready!" Benjamin's and Bugsy Wugsy's SHRILL voices shouted happily as they burst into the control room.

"Super!" I answered with a big smile. "Let's go!"

Even though I appeared excited, deep down, I was a little worried. I don't know about you, but those floating holograms make me nauseous! We got to the theater a little early, but it was already packed with mice munching on mouthwatering triple-cheese-flavored popcorn.

As soon as the lights dimmed, the seats began to float and *The Lord of the Asteroids* began. The movie was full of speeding space shuttles, evil aliens, and mouse-crushing meteorites.

SQUEAK! HOW TERRIFYING!

After a few minutes, the images suddenly started flickering and became *blurry*. Then the screen began to **VIBRATE**. "Uncle, is this a new special effect?" Benjamin asked.

Before I could answer, the movie suddenly cut out completely and we were plunged into **darkness**. It was darker than the blackest black hole!

A Near Miss!

Everyone became very quiet. I held BENJAMIN'S and **Bugsy Wugsy's** paws tightly in an attempt to reassure them, even though my whiskers trembled with *fear*. Then a small dot of light appeared in front of me. A second later, **HOLOGRAMIX**, *MouseStar 1*'s onboard computer, was beaming at me. I was so **surprised**, I almost jumped out of my seat!

"Red alert!
Red alert!
Red alert!"

Hologramix shouted. "Captain Stiltonix, report to the **control room** immediately!"

Red alert?! Since I had become captain, there had been only *yellow alerts*! A red alert means there is a supergalactic **CRISIS**! What could have happened?!

The theater's **lights** finally came back on. Benjamin, Bugsy Wugsy, and I **RUSHED** toward the exit and hurried to the control room. **Grandfather William Stiltonix** greeted me with his **booming**, incredibly intimidating voice.

"Grandson!" he barked. "Took you long **ENOUGh**! How can you be the captain of this spaceship if you're never around during an **emergency**?"

"Er . . . I—I was at the **movies** . . ." I stammered.

My grandfather became even more

INFURIATED.

"The **MOVIES**?!" he squeaked. "Do you realize our ship was almost **HIT** by a comet? Thanks to your sister's quick thinking, we still have the *fur* on our backs!"

Where were you?!

"A c-comet?" I squeaked. "How is that possible?"

"Let me explain, Captain," said our onboard scientist, **PROFESSOR GREENFUR**. "Our spaceship crossed the wake of comet **ALPHA 2093**, which appeared suddenly in our galaxy's quadrant."

"I had to *veer* at the last moment," my sister, Thea, explained. "But I still don't *understand* why the comet didn't show up on our alert system."

"The comet produced a **swarm** of small particles that interfered with our instruments," Professor Greenfur explained. "Basically, the comet caused a temporary **malfunction** in our equipment!"

Swarm?

Small particles?

Interference?

Luckily, Benjamin explained everything to me. He had taken a course in astronomy.

COMETS

Comets are made up of **ice**, **rocks**, and **dust**. When a comet comes near the sun, it heats up and becomes a glowing ball. The ice and dust change into a gas that forms a long, tail-like **trail** behind the glowing ball. Comets gradually disintegrate over time. The word **comet** comes from an ancient Greek word that means "a head with long hair."

"So will the COMET be disintegrating soon?" I asked, proud of my newfound knowledge.

"I'm afraid not," answered Professor Greenfur. "According to my calculations, Alpha 2093 will **disintegrate** in exactly 374 cosmic years!"

Trap clapped a paw on Thea's back.

According to my calculations . . .

"Nice work!" he said. "Now, anyone want to CELEBRATE our near miss with a little snack? I don't know about the rest of you, but I'm cosmically hungry!"

Yum!

I sighed. The only thing my cousin Trap ever seems to think about is eating!

"No, we can't leave our posts just yet," Professor Greenfur replied grimly. "We averted the DANGER, but another spaceship or planet could be in real trouble!"

Warning: Incoming Comet!

Professor Greenfur pressed a series of keys. An image of the comet appeared on the screen.

"Comets follow regular paths around the sun, just like planets," Professor Greenfur explained. "See this ring? That's the comet's ORBIT. I made some quick calculations, and look: There's going to be a CATASTROPHE!"

I stared at the screen, but I didn't know what he meant.

"Er . . . excuse me, Professor," I said, feeling a little embarrassed. "But I don't see anything dangerous here."

Grandfather William pointed to a **reddish** planet on the map.

"**Grandson**, can't you see that the comet's orbit will place it in the direct path of this **PLANE†**?"

"Yes, but that planet is at least **five times** bigger than the comet," Trap pointed out. "How can that **little old comet** damage such a big **planet**?"

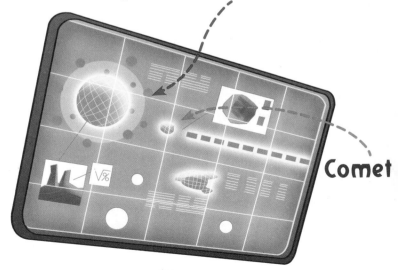

Comet

"Given the speed of the comet and its mass, it can do a lot of damage!" Professor Greenfur squeaked in dismay. "If you consider the friction of the atmosphere and the size, density, **velocity**, and angle of the comet, you'll see that the planet will EXPLODE on impact!"

It will explode!

A shiver of fear ran from the tips of my ears down to the end of my tail.

"How long until impact?" I asked.

"One day, seven hours, forty-six minutes, and twenty-seven astral seconds," the professor replied.

Black-holey galaxies! That

wasn't much time at all!

"Is the planet inhabited?" I squeaked.

This time, Hologramix answered.

"Yes, it is," the computer said. "It's the planet Jurassix, and it's inhabited by the cosmosaurs."

An image of a **cute** little alien appeared on the screen. It had a sweet, friendly face, **LARGE** eyes, and a tail shaped like a comma.

From the Encyclopedia Galactica

Planet: Jurassix
Location: Galaxy quadrant 24/765
Description: Has a dry, rocky surface
Inhabitants: Cosmosaurs
Language spoken: Saurese

A Rescue Mission

"The cosmosaurs seem so nice!" Benjamin squeaked softly. "Uncle G, we **TOTALLY** have to save them!"

Bugsy Wugsy nodded her head in **agreement**.

The mouselets were right. We had to do everything in our power to save those aliens!

"Contact the cosmosaurs immediately!" I ordered Hologramix.

"**Negative**, Captain," the computer answered. "According to the info in our archives, the cosmosaurs don't have the technology for **intergalactic communication**."

"I guess that means we'll have to warn

them **in the fur**," Trap said. "And I

I volunteer!

volunteer to go on the **mission**!
I'll bet there's something g⊙⊙d
to eat on that planet, and
I want to taste all the
cosmosaur specialties!"

"That's the **SPIRIT**,
Grandson!" Grandfather
William

Good for you, Grandson!

squeaked, clapping a paw
on Trap's back. "But
warning them isn't
enough. We have to
bring them on board
MOUSESTAR 1 if we
want to *save* them!"

"They can stay in the
spaceship's spare cabins until we find a new
planet for them to inhabit," Thea suggested.

"But what if the cosmosaurs don't want to leave their planet?" I asked, worried. "They may be too **scared**."

"It won't be a **problem**, Cuz," Trap said. "No one likes leaving his home, but it's better than getting hit on the head by a COMET!"

Trap wasn't wrong, but I was still concerned. Benjamin was hopeful, though.

"Uncle, didn't you see what gentle creatures the cosmosaurs are?" he said. "I bet they'll greet us with open paws!"

I gave in. I can never say no to my sweet little nephew. And we really had no other choice. We had to help the cosmosaurs, and we had **no time to spare**! In one day, seven hours, fourteen minutes, and thirty-three astral seconds the comet would make impact.

"Hurry up!" Grandfather William urged us. "The cosmosaur **rescue mission** is under way!"

But before we left, we had to take care of a few problems.

First: **How would we get to Jurassix?**

"Let's take my space shuttle," Thea suggested. "I saw a **FLAT** area on the map where I should be able to land **easily**!"

But there was another problem: **How would we communicate with the cosmosaurs?**

"Modestly speaking, I'm programmed to speak all **3,847** known languages in the galaxy," our multipurpose onboard robot, Robotix, declared **PROUDLY**. "Therefore, I know Saurese, the cosmosaur language."

"Are you sure?" Trap challenged him. "Prove it!"

Robotix then produced a series of incomprehensible **grumbling** sounds.

"What does that mean?" Trap asked.

"It means, 'You don't know if I can speak it or not, **Cheesehead**!'" Robotix replied.

Everyone except Trap burst out **LAUGHING**!

Finally, there was a third problem: **Who would go on the mission?**

Benjamin and Bugsy Wugsy came forward.

"Uncle, can we go?" they asked. "We'd like to join Trap and Robotix and help save the **cosmosaurs**!"

"I don't know," I replied, hesitating. "It could be dangerous . . ."

"And that's why you will go, too, Grandson!" Grandfather's voice boomed. "You'll be in charge of the mission! After all, you're the **captain**, aren't you?"

I sighed. The truth is, I would have preferred to spend the day relaxing *peacefully* in my cabin, but of course I couldn't. We were on a mission to save those **defenseless** aliens. And I was in **command**!

We **boarded** Thea's space shuttle, and in no **time** at all we had landed on Jurassix.

ANYBODY HOME?

Thea's space shuttle landed in a **DESERT** on Jurassix. Trap, Robotix, Benjamin, Bugsy Wugsy, and I all climbed out.

"This is where I'll pick you up," Thea told us. "I'm heading back to *MouseStar 1* to prepare for the **COSMOSAURS'** arrival. See you soon!"

We watched as the space shuttle **disappeared** in the distance. We were completely **alone** on an unfamiliar planet. Which way were we supposed to go? Stellar Swiss cheese! Why do I always have so much **trouble** reading astral maps?

Luckily, Benjamin came to my rescue.

"Do you need help, U̇n̈c̈l̈ë?" he asked sweetly.

"Er, yes," I admitted, embarrassed. "Thank you!"

"This dot is where we are," Benjamin said, pointing **CONFIDENTLY** to the map. "According to the map, the cosmosaur village is here. So we have to go *north*!"

Hmm . . . this way?
No, that way!

Ha!

Ha!

Bugsy Wugsy was so **EXCITED** she could barely stay in her fur.

"I can't wait to meet those **adorable** cosmosaurs!" she squeaked.

But instead of excitement, I felt a strange, **annoying** itchiness on my snout. I twitched my nose and we headed north.

After a while, we saw a narrow path between some **rocks**.

YOO-HOO!

"According to the map, we have to go **this way**," Benjamin explained.

Trap took a step forward.

"Yoo-hoo!" he shouted.

His voice echoed, but there was no reply.

Yoo-hooo ... Yoo-hoooo ... Yoo-hooooo . . .

YOO-HOO! YOO-HOO!

"Anybody home?" Trap continued.

Anybody home? Anybody home? Anybody home?

All of a sudden I had an **UNEASY** feeling.

"Stop it!" I told my cousin. "You might disturb —"

"Who?" Trap interrupted me with a chuckle. "Those cute little cosmosaurs?"

Suddenly, a huge **SHADOW** fell over us.

We turned and . . .

GALACTIC GORGONZOLA! A terrifying shape had appeared behind us. It had an **enormouse** face, two *tiny* arms, and a massive body that ended with a comma-shaped tail. Hey, wait a minute! It was IDENTICAL to the cosmosaur Hologramix had shown us, but it was much, much, much **bigger**! And it didn't

seem to have a **SWEET** disposition, either. In fact, this cosmosaur was downright scary!

The **alien** looked at us menacingly, baring its **SHARP** fangs. Benjamin, Bugsy Wugsy, and Robotix hid behind me in **fear**. Trap, on the other hand, wasn't scared at all.

"Relax!" he said calmly. "This guy is just a **little** bit bigger than we expected."

"You mean, **they're** a little bit bigger than we expected," I corrected him as three more cosmosaurs emerged from behind the rocks. The aliens **STARED** at us for a moment. Then another one bared its **fangs** and roared.

"Groooarrr! Grrrrr roooarrrg. Grrr groooaaar!"

"Wh-what is it saying, Robotix?" I asked in a shaky voice.

"They want to know who we are, WHERE we come from, and what we want!" Robotix replied quickly.

Trap stepped forward.

"Dear cosmosaur friends, we are a delegation of spacemice who have come to —"

The cosmosaurs didn't let him finish.

"Grooooaaar grrr!"

We all looked at Robotix.

"He said, 'You can explain what you're doing on our planet to our king,'" Robotix translated. "'He will decide what to do with you. Follow us!'"

IT WAS JUST A BABY!

We **followed** the cosmosaurs toward their village.

"Cousin, do you think we can **trust** them?" I whispered to Trap as we walked. "I really don't like the way they're **looking** at us!"

"We don't have a **CHOICE**," Trap replied. "We'll have to talk to their king and explain that they are in **DANGER**!"

"Yes, of course," I squeaked. "It's just that . . ."

"What?"

The itch on

AH . . . AH . . . ACHOOOOO!

my snout was **worse** than ever, and I couldn't hold back.

"AH...AH...AH...ACHOO!"

I exploded into a galactic sneeze that **startled** everyone!

"Uncle, you frightened him!" Benjamin scolded me. "Try to sneeze more **QUiETLY** next time!"

"But who did I **frighten**?" I asked, perplexed.

"Him!" Benjamin replied. He pointed to a **LiTTLE** cosmosaur who was scampering on the path by the rocks.

I suddenly realized our **MISTAKE**. The image of the cosmosaur we had seen on board the *MouseStar 1* had been a picture of a **baby**!

"Uncle G, can we say **hello** to him?" Bugsy Wugsy asked.

I hesitated. "Well, I suppose so," I said. "But be very *careful*!"

But Benjamin and Bugsy Wugsy were already **running** toward the little creature. After a moment's hesitation, the tiny alien came closer and was now letting them **scratch** his tummy!

"Look how **nice** he is!" Benjamin exclaimed.

"He's so **sweet**!" added Bugsy Wugsy.

"Grrff frrrrr frrrrfrrrr . . ."

He's so nice!

"He says his name is FRED!" Robotix translated.

"Hi, Fred!" exclaimed Bugsy Wugsy.

The little cosmosaur licked Benjamin's and Bugsy Wugsy's faces, making them GIGGLE with delight.

Martian mozzarella!

The three of them had already become friends!

Meanwhile, Robotix and Trap were walking beside the adult COSMOSAURS. Unfortunately, they seemed a lot less friendly than the baby. I could hear Trap squeaking about food, as always.

"So, what are the special dishes served on your planet?" Trap asked.

The cosmosaur licked his fangs and growled to Robotix.

"'You'll find out soon!'" he translated. "'To celebrate your visit, our king will have a **banquet** in your honor!'"

Trap smiled at me.

"See?" he boasted. "They're very POLITE! I told you there was **nothing** to be afraid of! Robotix, tell them we'd be hONORED to attend their feast. And ask them what the specialty is. I'm very curious!"

As soon as Robotix finished translating, the cosmosaurs burst out LAUGHING. Trap and I LOOKED at each other, perplexed. What was so funny?

Bow to the King!

A few minutes later, we **ARRIVED** in a circular clearing with a **small lake** at its center. All around us were high rocks with caves opening onto the clearing. There were signs hanging all around, which Robotix translated. One read, "**CLAW SHARPENING**" and another read, "**SPEAR TRAINING**."

Squeak! For some reason, that place really gave me the creeps!

On one side of the clearing an enormouse cosmosaur looked down from a **HUGE** stone throne.

"Could that be their **KING**?" Trap asked me.

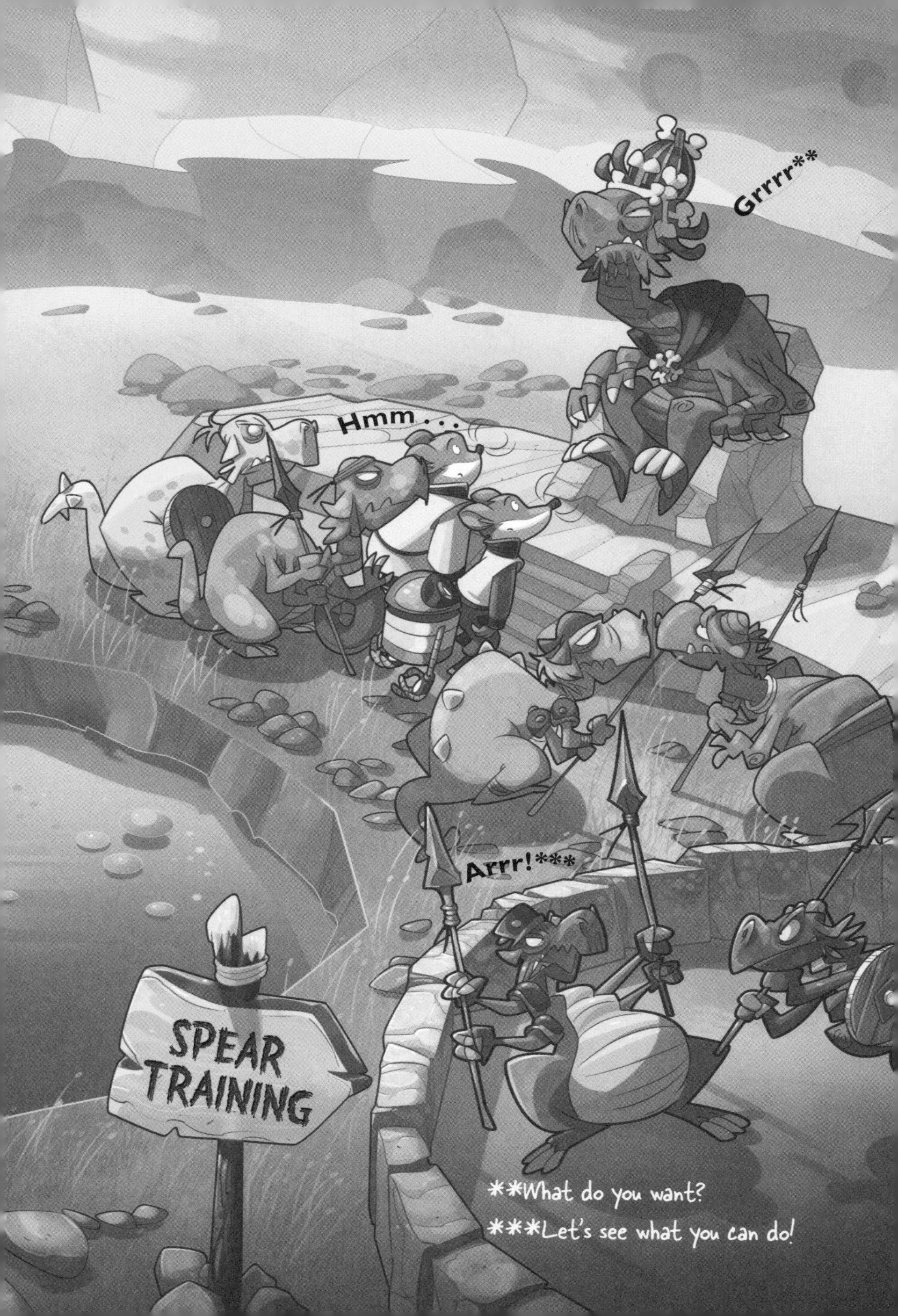

**What do you want?

***Let's see what you can do!

Mmmmm . . . *

*Mmmmm . . .

I took a better look and saw that the alien on the throne was wearing a crown of **little bones** on his head! A shiver ran down my fur . . .

The cosmosaur got up and addressed us through Robotix.

"I am King Rex the Sixteenth," he said. "Welcome to Jurassix. I'm so pleased to see foreigners who are so HEALTHY and PLUMP!"

"What does that mean?" Trap grumbled. "I went on a diet last week!"

"My name is Captain Stiltonix," I replied slowly so my squeak wouldn't shake with fear. "My friends and I come from the spaceship *MouseStar 1*. We are here on a **rescue mission.** A comet is heading this way! It will **destroy** your planet in exactly one day!"

"That's *impossible!*" the king roared. "In one day is the **Feast of the Hot Sun!**"

"Er, okay," I replied. "I'm not sure what that is, but you really must **evacuate** Jurassix as soon as possible! One of our **space shuttles** is ready to —"

"That's enough!" the king interrupted me with a growl. "This conversation is **BORING** me!"

"Er, maybe the captain didn't explain himself thoroughly," Trap piped up. "The comet is on a **trajectory** that will cross your planet's orbit. You have to *leave* here immediately!"

"And where should we go, **mouse?**" the king asked **indignantly.**

"F-for now, you could be guests on our ship," I replied hesitantly. I really didn't tRuSt this king! "But we will definitely help you find another planet to live on."

The king seemed INTRIGUED by my offer.

"Another planet?" he said thoughtfully. "Well, well. It would be iNtEREStiNG to have two planets at one's disposal instead of just one. I'll think about it!"

Then he ordered us to leave.

Trap and I LOOKED at each other, perplexed. Was it possible the cosmosaur didn't understand the danger he and his fellow aliens were in?

"I'm afraid you can't think about it," I squeaked timidly. "You have to act right now if—"

"Enough!" The king roared, baring his fangs. "I give the commands around here!

And I command that the Feast of the Hot Sun will go on whether the planet is destroyed or not! Subject closed!"

The rest of the cosmosaurs roared in approval. The king gestured for silence.

"Now, take our, er, guests away!" he ordered. "I have to rest. Tomorrow we will have a banquet of . . . what did you say you were again? Ah, yes — roasted **spacemice**!"

Wh–what? Had I heard him correctly? A banquet of roasted spacemice?!

"Are you sure you translated that correctly?" I asked Robotix. "We're here to save them and they want to eat us? There must be a **mistake**!"

"No, that's what he said," the little robot answered **iRRiTaBLY**. "I don't make mistakes, Captain!"

Trap and I exchanged a glance. In a split

second, I made a **decision**.

"**We have to ruuuuuun!**" I shouted.

Trap and I grabbed Benjamin's and Bugsy Wugsy's paws and **ran**. Robotix followed close behind us. But in no time, a cosmosaur **grabbed** us and pulled us into one of the caves. Then he ordered two other cosmosaurs to stand in front of the cave and keep us from **escaping**!

MOUSEY METEORITES! We were done for!

Help!

AH . . . AH . . . ACHOO!

I began to **TREMBLE** from the tips of my ears to the end of my tail. We were **prisoners** of aliens who wanted to gobble us up, and there was a **COMET** headed straight for us!

"Uncle?" Benjamin's voice interrupted my thoughts. "What are we going to do now?"

At that exact moment, my wrist phone **beeped**. It was Thea calling from *MouseStar 1*!

"Come in, Captain," she said. "How's the mission going? Have you warned the **COSMOSAURS**?"

"You could say that," I replied. "We *warned* them, and they **captured** us!"

"Captured?!" Thea gasped. "But why?"

"Well, it turns out the cosmosaurs aren't CUTE and cuddly like we thought. They're enormouse and hungry, and they want to ROAST and eat us!"

"What?!" Thea replied. "That means something's wrong with the ENCYCLOPEDIA GALACTICA. And it's the captain's duty to make sure we're using the most updated version."

Huh?! The captain's duty? OOPS.

"Um, well, I guess I FORGOT to do that . . ." I muttered under my whiskers.

"So we ventured to this planet thinking we'd find friendly aliens, and instead we found mice-munching MONSTERS!" Trap squeaked angrily.

My snout turned bright red with embarrassment. This mess was all my fault!

"Please, let's not argue now," Benjamin interrupted us. "We've got to come up with an **escape** plan!"

"That's right!" Thea agreed through my wrist phone. "In the meantime, I'll get the space shuttle ready to pick you up."

Trap sat down on a ROCK so that he could calm down a bit. A minute later . . . **drriiiip**! A drop of water fell on his head.

"That's it!" Trap exclaimed suddenly. "If water is dripping from the ceiling, that means there's an opening somewhere!"

We all looked UP.

Huh?

There was a tiny hole in the wall of the cave where water and a feeble flicker of light came through.

"Yes!" cheered Trap. "We can get out!"

"But how?" Benjamin protested. "That hole is so HIGH."

"I'll take care of it!" Robotix said proudly. "This is a job for a highly **advanced** robotic being. Namely, me!"

He took out a propeller, activated the flight mode, and lifted himself up a couple of inches from the **ground**.

"I'll go up first," he explained. "Then I'll lift each of you up with my MECHANICAL ARMS!"

That sounded perfect! It was an excellent plan, except for the fact that right at that moment . . . ,

"**Ah . . . ah . . . achoo!**"

I exploded in a huge **sneeze**. Then I lost my **BALANCE** and landed right on top of the little robot.

CRUNCH!

Robotix tipped over and his propeller blade **cracked**!

"Geronimo!" Trap **moaned**. "Look what you just did!"

"I'm so sorry," I **whispered**. "When my snout **ITCHES**

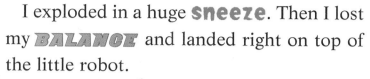

like that, I just can't control myself!"

As if that weren't enough, my galactic sneeze had attracted the ATTENTiON of the two cosmosaurs at the entrance to the cave. They turned toward us menacingly.

"What's going on in there?" they asked. (Robotix continued to TRaNSLaTe for us.)

"Oh, nothing," I replied nonchalantly. "We're just EXERCiSiNG a bit!"

But the two COSMOSaUrS didn't buy it.

"Yeah?" one of them replied. "Well, we think you were trying to escape!"

The other one pointed to the hole at the top of the cave.

Holey craters! They were on to us!

One of them immediately rolled a giant **boulder** in front of the hole. Then the aliens sat in front of the entrance to the cave and began to SNORE.

I'LL CATCH YOU!

When **DARKNESS** fell, Benjamin turned on the light on his wrist phone.

"Luckily, we've got these," he squeaked.

The beam of light **lit up** the cave wall, illuminating the den where we were being held captive. I, too, lit my wrist phone, but I aimed it in the wrong DIRECTION. Instead of the wall, the light hit my snout, **blinding** me for a second!

I **staggered** around the cave,

accidentally flashing the light all around me.

"Be careful, Uncle G!" Benjamin warned. "You're going to wake up the cosmosaurs!" But it was too late.

The two aliens guarding the cave opened their *eyes*. We cowered in **fear**, wondering what they would do **NEXT**. But they didn't even seem to **notice** us! Instead, they focused on the beam of light. Then they stretched out their sharp claws and tried to **CATCH** it!

"What are they doing?" Trap whispered.

STELLAR SWISS!

I didn't have a clue!

"It looks like they're **attracted** to the light," I replied.

"That's it!" Bugsy Wugsy squeaked. "We can use the **light** to escape!"

"What do you mean?" I asked, perplexed.

"I get it!" Benjamin said, pointing his wrist phone's **LIGHT** at a spot on the wall near the two cosmosaurs. The aliens got up and began **CHASING** after the light.

"They follow the light as if it's *prey*," Bugsy Wugsy explained.

Galactic Gorgonzola!

Now I understood! We could trick the aliens into following the light around instead of **guarding** the entrance to the cave. Then we would be able to **slip** past them!

Without losing a moment, we put our plan into **Action**. We activated the light on one of our wrist phones and attached it to a **root** hanging from the cave's ceiling.

The **beam** of light reached the ground beyond the entrance to the cave! The first cosmosaur ran after the , and soon the second alien followed the first. Quickly and quietly as mice, we scampered out of the cave undisturbed.

Gggrrr!*

*I'll catch you!

Run, Geronimo, Run!

As soon as we had escaped, I called Thea.

"We got away!"

"Stellar Swiss, that's great!" she exclaimed. "I'll wait for you with my shuttle at the same **SPOT** I left you!"

We followed the directions on the map and hightailed it down the **rocky** path. In seconds I was out of breath, my legs burned, and my paws were so heavy it felt as if I was running on two wheels of **melted Martian cheese.**

I didn't think I would be able to make it back to the shuttle! But then I heard Benjamin's sweet voice encouraging me.

"Just a little farther, Uncle!" he squeaked helpfully. "We're almost there. Look!"

There it was! Thea's shuttle was waiting for us. The hatch was open and the engine was running! We were saved!

But suddenly a strange feeling washed over me, setting my fur on edge. I felt as though someone — or something — was WATCHING us. How weird.

I looked to my right as I ran, but there was nothing there. Still, I felt the strange presence. very weird.

Then I looked left, but there was still nothing. very, very weird.

Finally, I glanced behind me. HOLEY

CRATERS! A pair of **bright** yellow eyes was staring right at me.

Wait a minute — it wasn't just **one** pair of eyes. No, there were **TEN** pairs!

Martian mozzarella! That's **twenty** eyes!

With what little breath I had left, I **shouted** to my friends.

"The cosmosaurs . . . **PUFF** . . . are right . . . **pant** . . . behind us!" I yelled. "Run as fast as you **CAAAAAN!**"

There was only one small **hill** between me and the shuttle. But I could feel a cosmosaur's **hot** breath on my fur. The alien was trying to **bite** my tail! I began running in a **zigzag** so he wouldn't **catch** me.

Meanwhile, Trap, Benjamin, Bugsy Wugsy, and Robotix had already climbed **safely** inside the shuttle. They **cheered** me on,

*If I catch you . . .   **You're done for, mouse!

but I was losing steam. I turned for a second and saw the sharp, pointy fangs of the cosmosaur right BEHIND me. I thought I was a goner for sure!

Then things got even **worse**!

I felt a little tickle on my snout, just below my whiskers. A second later . . .

"AAAAAAAACHOOOO!"

The force of the sneeze made me close my eyes, and I **tripped** on a rock. Luckily, I went flying forward and sailed through the shuttle's open hatch. I was **saved**!

As soon as I realized my fur was safe at last, you guessed it — I fainted!

NEVER GIVE UP!

When I woke up, we were back on board
MOUSESTAR 1.

"Mmmm," I murmured. "What's
that delicious smell?"

"It's Cook Squizzy's **galactic
Gorgonzola** extract!" Trap
explained. "I told him if he held
the bottle open under your nose,
you'd come to **immediately**!"

"Are you okay, Uncle G?"
Benjamin asked worriedly.

"Now that we're all *safe*, I'm fine," I
exclaimed as I gave my nephew a big hug. "I
just gave myself a bit of a **bump**!"

I touched the LUMP on the top of my head.

"Whew!" I sighed. "We had a close call losing those — **Aaaaaachooo!**"

I exploded into a cosmic sneeze.

"That's the same kind of sneeze I had on planet Jurassix," I mused. "How weird!"

"Not really," Trap chuckled. "It's clear, dear cousin, that you are **allergic** to Jurassix rock moss!"

"That can't be!" I replied. "There's no moss here."

Trap smiled and **pointed** behind me.

"There's no **moss**, but there's one of **those**," he said. "Maybe he's got some moss stuck in his claws!"

I turned around to see the cosmosaur that had been chasing me sitting in the corner!

"Arrrgh!" I squeaked. "Heeelp! Run!"

"Calm down, Geronimo!" Trap said. "Can't you see he's **sound asleep**?"

I wasn't convinced, so I approached him **slowly**. As I got closer, I saw he was tied up with a **thick** rope. I pulled his tail, but the alien didn't move! However, I began to sneeze all over again!

"Ah . . . ah . . . achoooo!"

Then I asked, "What's he doing here?"

"When you **flew** into the shuttle, Thea immediately closed the hatch, but he had already jumped inside after you, **smacking** his head against the wall!" Benjamin explained.

What's he doing here?

ZZZZZZZZZ . . .

"And just like you, he fainted on the spot!" Bugsy Wugsy added with a giggle.

"B-but what happens if he wakes up?" I asked, my whiskers **shaking**.

"Can't you see we **tied** him up so tight he can't get away?" Trap asked.

I breathed a huge **sigh** of relief. But a moment later, Benjamin reminded us that we still had a **BIG** problem. In fact, it was *comet-sized*!

"We still haven't completed our mission," Benjamin said. "Even though the cosmosaurs wanted to **eat** us, we can't let them be smashed by that comet."

"And besides, our friend **FRED** is still on Jurassix," Bugsy Wugsy added.

I sighed. I thought about that sweet baby cosmosaur and knew we had to *do* something. **BUT WHAT?**

"You're right!" I told my nephew and his friend. **"We have to find a solution!"**

Grandfather William cleared his throat from across the room.

"Good for you, Grandson!" he squeaked. "For once you said the right thing! *Spacemice* never give up! It's our duty to help any inhabitants in the galaxy who are in **danger**, even if they are less than **friendly**!"

His words **cheered** us and gave us courage. We weren't going to **GIVE UP**!

What Can We Do?

Suddenly, I heard a **noise** in the background.

"Trap, did you say **something**?" I asked.

"No," he replied. "I didn't say a *thing*!"

"**Grrrrrrrrowl . . .**"

"What was that, Benjamin?" I asked.

"Nothing, Uncle!"

"**Grrrrrrooowwwl . . .**"

My whiskers quivered. **Solar-smoked Gouda!** The cosmosaur was awake!

I asked Robotix to translate for me.

"Er . . . Hello, c-cosmosaur," I squeaked **nervously**. "You are on the spaceship *MouseStar 1.*"

"Grrrrrrowl roooooooarrrr grrrrrrooowl groarrr!"

"He says if he gets free, he'll eat everyone up!" Robotix translated.

Gulp! I swallowed and continued anyway.

"Well, uh, as I was saying, you don't have to be frightened because —"

"Grrrrowl rooooooarrrr!"

he said, interrupting me.

I turned toward Robotix.

"He says we're the ones who should be trembling with **FRIGHT**!" the robot said.

"Well, okay, but

perhaps you *misunderstood*," I tried again. "We came to your planet to help you —"

"**Grrrrrrrrrowl roooarrrrr grrrrrooowl!**"

"He says to take him back to Jurassix now, or we'll be in **deep** trouble!"

"These cosmosaurs are so **stubborn**!" I said with a sigh. "Hologramix, activate external visualization!"

An image appeared on the screen **immEDiATELY.**

"That's your planet right there," I explained **patiently**. "See that comet? It's ZOOMiNG toward Jurassix! It's going to **crash** right into your planet! If you'd just **relax** for

a moment, you'd see that we're only trying to *help* you."

The alien stopped **fidgeting** instantly and stared at us. Maybe he **finally** understood the danger his fellow cosmosaurs were in!

"**Growl** . . ." he whispered softly.

"He says he's sorry . . ." Robotix translated.

"**Grrr. Prrr prrr.**"

"His name is Reginald, and he wants to work with us to **SAVE** his fellow aliens!"

We agreed to free Reginald if he promised not to **eat** us. Then we went to find Sally de Wrench, the ship's official mechanic. She's a truly **clever** rodent who always has great *ideas*. She's also one of the nicest rodents on board the *MouseStar 1*!

Sally wanted to calculate the **trajectory** of the comet down to the tiniest detail. She thought that might give us some ideas as to how we could **STOP** it. But we were running out of *time*. We had to get the other cosmosaurs off Jurassix, and we had to do it *quickly*!

"Why don't we go back to Jurassix with Reginald?" Benjamin suggested. "He'll **CONVINCE** everyone there that they have to follow us onto our spaceship if they want to *survive!*"

Thea shook her head.

"There's no time to **transport** them all," she explained. "They're too **LARGE**! We would need to make at least **ten** trips on the space shuttle, and we only have six hours left before the comet's **impact**! We'll never make it!"

"So what in **space** are we going to do?" I asked. We were out of **ideas**, and almost out of **TIME**!

I HAVE THE
SOLUTION!

Suddenly, a commotion behind us got our attention. **PROFESSOR GREENFUR** had just come running into the **control room**.

"Professor, where have you been?" Trap asked him. "We could really use your help."

"I was in my *laboratory* making some calculations," the scientist explained as he caught his breath. "I have the solution that will save the cosmosaurs!"

We all gasped. What **fabumouse** news!

"Well, what is it?" I asked, eagerly awaiting his reply.

"We need to calculate the speed of the **comet** and its rocky mass and compare it with the dimensions of our **spaceship**. Then we have to multiply the **power** of our engines by the force of the comet, divide by the **length** of the hangar, and —"

As usual, I didn't have a **clue** what he was squeaking about!

"Er, Professor, we're in a bit of a hurry," I said, interrupting him. "What's the solution?"

He looked me right in the snout.

The solution is . . .

"Well, it's obvious, isn't it?" he said. "We need to seize the comet and shift its trajectory!"

Trap burst out laughing.

"That's funny!" he guffawed. "And how are we going to grab and shift a comet?"

Before Professor Greenfur could answer, Sally squeaked up.

"But of course!" she cried. "We'll use a huge space net!"

"Exactly!" Professor Greenfur confirmed. "THEA will take *MouseStar 1* as close as possible to the comet so that SALLY can launch the space net. Once the comet is harnessed to our ship, we'll set our engines on warp speed so we can move its trajectory to exactly 7.64921 degrees! After that, we can set it free to follow its own course."

"But where will the comet go?" Benjamin

asked dubiously.

Professor Greenfur tapped the control panel and an image of a *bleak*, **isolated** asteroid appeared on the screen.

"The comet will head toward the asteroid Solitarius, which is completely devoid of life. Then there will be a galactic explosion!"

"Okay, spacemice!" Grandfather William exclaimed. "Everyone, get to your posts. Let's start operation rescue!"

"**Grrrrrrrrrroowl!**" Reginald said.

We didn't need a translation to understand that he was very happy with our new idea!

GROOOWL

CAST THE
SPACE NET!

Thea immediately began planning the complicated maneuver of getting **near** the comet. First she double-checked the **coordinates** Professor Greenfur had provided. Then she began to fly the *MouseStar 1* straight toward the comet!

From the control room, I looked out the *window* and saw the comet right in front of us. Its **smoky halo** and **silvery tail** were truly beautiful. We moved closer and closer, until suddenly the ship came to a halt with a *jolt*.

Beep! Beeeep! Beeeeep!

An alarm sounded.

"Why did we stop, Thea?" I asked, worried.

"We're getting too close to the comet, Captain," she replied. "From now on, I'll have to proceed with manual controls. Otherwise our ship might be **damaged**!"

A second later, Thea began guiding the *MouseStar 1* manually. Suddenly, the ship began to tremble.

"Wh-what's happening now?" I squeaked. Black-holey galaxies . . . I wasn't sure my nerves could take much more of this. I felt like I was inside a blender!

"We're experiencing some turbulence due to our proximity to the comet," Thea replied. "But everything's under control!"

I trusted my sister completely, but I really hoped the SHAKING would stop soon!

"Activate the position stabilizers!" Thea squeaked.

The situation improved instantly, and the turbulence became just a mild vibration.

"We'll have to be quick!" Thea said, a worried look on her snout. "It's difficult to stay this close to the comet for long. Plus the stabilizers use a lot of ENERGY! Let's go ahead and cast the space net!"

3...2...1...
CAST OFF!

Sally was already in position. She began the countdown:

"5 . . . 4 . . . 3 . . . 2 . . . 1 . . . CAST OFF!"

We watched the space net *fly* toward the comet, its superstellar cable tethering it to our ship. The launch seemed to have gone well, but I waited for Sally to give me the signal.

"The launch has . . . *failed*!" Sally squeaked. "I repeat: The space net did not reach the comet."

Martian mozzarella! What a disappointment!

We were all upset by the news, but Reginald was especially distraught.

"*Grooooar*," he moaned **unhappily**.

"We'll try **again**," Trap reassured him. "You'll see. This time we'll do it!"

"Recover the net!" I ordered. "Prepare for the second launch!"

We held our breath as Sally prepared to launch the net again.

Thea realigned the *MouseStar 1* with the comet and began the countdown:

"5 . . . 4 . . . 3 . . . 2 . . . 1 . . . Cast off!"

Sally cast the net.

We watched the net fly out again, waiting with QUIVERING whiskers for Sally's word.

"The launch has failed!" Sally said. "I repeat: The launch has failed!"

The command room grew very **QUIET**. Then Reginald burst out in a **desperate** moan. I ran to **CONSOLE** him. He hugged me tightly and began to cry, **spurting** tears like a fountain. In less than a minute, my uniform was sopping **wet**.

Boo hoo hoo!

I couldn't believe that just a few hours earlier, Reginald had been about to eat me for lunch!

"So, what do we do NOW?" Benjamin asked quietly.

"There's got to be another way to shift that PESKY comet!" Bugsy Wugsy replied, a determined look on her snout.

Professor Greenfur looked at the mouselets and then rested his gaze on me.

"Captain, there is one other possibility," he said seriously. "We can secure the net MANUALLY!"

THE LAST RESORT

There are times when the captain has to show he's a real **leader**. At these times, everyone counts on the captain to make the right decision in a **stressful** situation.

This was one of those times!

"**GRANDSON!**" my grandfather barked. "**WHY** are you still standing there? **Take action!** Hurry up and put on your **spacesuit**. We have a planet to save! Snap to it!

Take action!

Snap! Snaaaaaap!"

Grandfather William's booming voice penetrated my thoughts.

"Got it, Grandson?" he shouted again.

Of course I got it! The only way to save Jurassix from destruction was for me to fly out into space and manually harness the net around the comet. And everything had to be done incredibly QUICKLY because the comet was going to CRASH into Jurassix in less than an hour!

I knew what I had to do, but truth be told, I was scared. I would have to go out into deep space all by MYSELF!

Luckily, Thea seemed to sense my fear.

"Okay, I'm ready," she announced calmly. "I'm going with you, Geronimo!"

What a brave and courageous sister I had! Still, I continued to tremble with fear. The mission in space was going to be very, very **dangerous**!

"Uncle, we have **FaiTh** in you!" squeaked a **reassuring** little voice. It was Benjamin, of course. "You're the best uncle in the whole **universe**!"

You can do it, Ger!

Ahhh, my sweet little nephew. What would I do without him?

Before I could change my mind, I put on my spacesuit and headed toward the exit **hatch**.

Just as I was about to open the door, I felt a **HUGE** claw clamp down on my shoulder. I turned and saw an enormouse tear **SLiDiNG** down Reginald's worried face.

"Grrooowwl roar frrrr!"

Growl!*

*I'm sorry!

"He says he's moved by the great **risk** you are taking to save his planet," Robotix translated. "Also, he's sorry he tried to eat you."

I smiled at him. "Well, we all make mistakes!"

A Walk
in Space

When the **hatch** first opened, I was paralyzed with fear. The comet was right in front of me, but beyond that was **outer space**! As a spacemouse, I had gone through six galactic months of training to learn how to use my **special** spacesuit, how to **WALK** and **float** in space, and even how to make **BASIC** repairs to the *MouseStar 1*. But it had been a long time since I had gone through training. Now that I needed to use those **skills**, I couldn't remember a **thing**!

I heard a **VOICE** through my helmet's headphones.

"Hurry up, Geronimo," Thea squeaked.

Er . . .

"**JUMP!**"

"O-okay, I'm coming!" I tried to sound **confident**, but I was so scared my legs felt as soft as Brie! I took a deep breath and jumped into space! Then I activated the small motor on my spacesuit that would allow me to **move** around. But when I pushed the button, I jolted forward, losing my balance! Suddenly, I was hanging **upside down**! **Solar-smoked Gouda!** I couldn't turn around!

"Ger, what are you doing?" Thea asked.

Jump, Ger!

Help!

Oooh!

Er...

"To regain your **equilibrium**, you just have to **MOVE** your arms!"

I began **flapping** my arms and legs like crazy. After a lot of effort, I finally got back into a vertical position. Then Thea and I moved toward the comet together. But a moment later, I found myself inside a cloud of stardust. I couldn't even **see** my own whiskers!

Galactic Gorgonzola!

I was lost in space!

"Thea, where are you?" I shouted into my space helmet.

"I'm right in front of you," she replied. "Don't you **see** me? Come **forward** slowly!"

Slowly? That was easier said than done! I could barely hold myself upright, much less **control** my speed. In fact, I inadvertently turned up the speed of the motor in my spacesuit. I **took off** like a bolt of lightning and smacked right into my sister!

"OOOF! SORRY!"

"Well, at least we found each other," Thea said. "From now on, hold on to me. We can't afford to l̄○s€ each other!"

A few minutes later, we found ourselves right in front of the **ENORMOUSE** comet.

"Take out the space net," Thea instructed me. "We're close enough to launch it now!"

I turned and saw that the comet was very, very close to Jurassix.

"I hope this works," I whispered to myself, crossing my paws for good **luck**.

A Speck of Moss Dust

Thea and I floated on either side of the comet, ready to **launch** the space net.

"We're almost there, Ger!" Thea said. "I'll throw the net around the comet, and you'll have to tighten it —"

Suddenly, sparks shot out of the **comet**. One of them hit Thea, and she dropped the net. I was able to retrieve it quickly, but Thea wasn't responding. She had **fainted**! I shook her and shook her until she came to.

"Would you please stop **shaking** me

like a cream cheese milkshake?" she said in a wobbly voice.

I breathed a deep sigh of relief.

"I'm so glad you're **OKAY**!" I replied. "You gave me a real *galactic* fright!"

"I'm okay, except my paws feel a little **numb**," she admitted. "I must have gotten too close to the comet and been **HiT** by the sparks."

"I have to take you right back to the **MOUSESTAR 1**!" I told her.

"No," Thea said firmly. "We don't have time. You must get the net on the comet **quickly**. Otherwise everything we've done so far is for nothing! **Come on!**"

I SIGHED.

I knew my sister was right. But would I be able to do it by **myself**? I thought again of Benjamin and Bugsy Wugsy, and of

Launching net!

Reginald's B⁙G, worried eyes. There was no question about it. It was up to me to **save the planet**!

I couldn't possibly let the spacemice — or the cosmosaurs — down. So I picked up the space net once more, **shook** it out, and tried to center it on the comet. But I lost my equilibrium and began **rolling** around again!

"Be strong, Ger," Thea said encouragingly. "You can do it!"

She was right. I *could* do it! I managed to stop **spinning**. Then I gathered all my **strength** and picked up the space net. Suddenly, what looked like a **tiny** speck of Jurassix moss dust floated in front of me and landed on my nose. I felt the usual ITCH . . .

"**Oh no!**" I squeaked. "**No, no, no. Not now!**

"**Aaaaachooooo!**"

The sneeze made me lose my balance **again**! I started rolling head over tail. When I regained control, I couldn't believe my **eyes**. The comet was perfectly wrapped and harnessed inside the space net!

"You rock, Ger!" Thea exclaimed. "That was *perfectly executed*! Now let's get back to the space shuttle. We have a comet to tow away from Jurassix!"

I took Thea's arm. Then we followed the safety CABLE all the way back to *MouseStar 1.*

ENGINES ON!
FULL SPEED AHEAD!

When our paws were firmly planted back on the *MouseStar 1*, we were greeted with a big cheer. But the mission wasn't complete yet: We still had to **tow the comet** away from Jurassix.

"Spacemice, to your posts!" I ordered. "There's no time to lose! Engines on! Full speed ahead!"

The **DISPLAY** signaled that

we had exactly **four minutes and fifty-two seconds** before the comet **crashed** into Jurassix!

"Roger that, Captain!" Thea replied.

Then she revved up the engines to full speed. We looked out the window and saw that the net was *stretching*! Would it hold?

What if the comet was too hEaVy for the *MouseStar 1* to move?

What if the professor had made a MISTAKE in his calculations? What if . . .

Suddenly, the ship began to inch forward . . .

But Professor Greenfur was worried.

"The engines are working too **hard**," he said anxiously. "The comet is too **heavy**!"

"Thea, give it more **power**!" I shouted.

Vrrrrroooor

Black-holey galaxies!

Everything began to TREMBLE. I held on tightly to my seat so I wouldn't **roll** to the floor! The comet was now very, very close to Jurassix. The countdown clock showed just **one minute** remaining before impact . . . Then **fifty seconds**!

Forty . . . thirty . . . twenty . . . ten . . .

Vrrrrrooooommmm!

mmm!

MouseStar 1 suddenly **ACCELERATED**, pulling the comet along with it. Then the comet began to **SPIN**. At that point, we released the space net. The comet moved away from us like an enormouse top, **whirling** wildly toward the asteroid Solitarius.

"In a few minutes, the comet will **hit** Solitarius," Professor Greenfur announced. "Come, **look**!"

We all held our breath as we looked out the window, waiting for the comet and the asteroid to **collide**.

BOOOOOOMMM!

A golden cloud of **space dust** rose from the collision as thousands of sparks streaked across space.

Wow! What a show!

It was as if we were watching an exhibition of interplanetary **fireworks**!

"Uncle G, this is even better than a 5-D mega mouserific movie, isn't it?" Benjamin whispered as he hugged me tightly.

"It sure is!" I answered my little nephew with a SMILE.

I had already **forgotten** that this entire adventure had started just one day ago at the movie theater. So much had happened since then that it seemed as if an entire lunar century had gone by. But most important, we had accomplished our goal: Jurassix was finally safe!

PUT YOUR PAW HERE!

Thea slowed **MOUSESTAR 1'S** engines. Mission accomplished! We had done it. We hugged one another **happily**.

Robotix and I approached Reginald.

"We did it," I told him. "Your planet is **safe**!"

He looked at me suspiciously.

"Grrrowlll frooar?" he roared **softly**.

"He's asking if you're sure," translated Robotix.

"Absolutely!" I replied, smiling at him. "The **comet** will no longer be a danger to anyone!"

The cosmosaur breathed a **SIGH** of relief.

"Spacemice, you've saved my planet," he said through Robotix. "You're **awesome**! Put your *paw* here!"

He took my paw and **squeezed** it so hard he almost C R U S H E D it!

Thea turned the ship and headed to Jurassix to take Reginald home. This time, the COSMOSAURS welcomed us like heroes. They had seen the

Grrr grrr!*

*Thank you!

comet **crash** into Solitarius. Reginald explained we were the ones who had **changed** the comet's course and saved their home!

Benjamin and Bugsy Wugsy found their little friend Fred with a bunch of other cute, gentle baby cosmosaurs. When we were all gathered together, King Rex the Sixteenth made a speech.

"I want to thank our new friends, the **spacemice**," he said. "They saved us from that **terrible** comet!"

"**ROOOOAAAR!**" shouted all the cosmosaurs.

"Of course, a nice banquet of spacemice would have been delicious," the king continued. **Mousey meteorites!** Not the banquet again! "But let's not dwell on that! We can finally celebrate the Feast of the Hot Sun. Let's start the festivities immediately!"

"**Rooooaaarrr!**" the rest of the cosmosaurs replied.

Then they broke out into a spirited dance around the fire. Luckily, Professor Greenfur had given me an antidote to my moss allergy. I was able to enjoy the festivities without a single nose itch!

*Good rhythm!
**Mmm! Smells good!

After the dancing, it was time for the games. Catch the Light appeared to be the cosmosaurs' favorite new form of entertainment. They chased a light projected on the side of a rock wall. But no one ever WON because the light couldn't be caught! Still, the cosmosaurs had a great time.

Soon it was late, and we needed to leave

our new **friends**. I couldn't wait to get back to the spaceship so that I could write about our incredible **adventure** on Jurassix. That's right! It's the **book** that's in your paws **right now**. I hope you enjoyed it!

See you on our next intergalactic adventure!

Don't miss any adventures of the Spacemice!

#1 Alien Escape

#2 You're Mine, Captain!

#3 Ice Planet Adventure

#4 The Galactic Goal

#5 Rescue Rebellion

Up Next!

#6 The Underwater Planet

Be sure to read all my fabumouse adventures!

#1 Lost Treasure of the Emerald Eye

#2 The Curse of the Cheese Pyramid

#3 Cat and Mouse in a Haunted House

#4 I'm Too Fond of My Fur!

#5 Four Mice Deep in the Jungle

#6 Paws Off, Cheddarface!

#7 Red Pizzas for a Blue Count

#8 Attack of the Bandit Cats

#9 A Fabumouse Vacation for Geronimo

#10 All Because of a Cup of Coffee

#11 It's Halloween, You 'Fraidy Mouse!

#12 Merry Christmas, Geronimo!

#13 The Phantom of the Subway

#14 The Temple of the Ruby of Fire

#15 The Mona Mousa Code

#16 A Cheese-Colored Camper

#17 Watch Your Whiskers, Stilton!

#18 Shipwreck on the Pirate Islands

#19 My Name Is Stilton, Geronimo Stilton

#20 Surf's Up, Geronimo!

#21 The Wild, Wild West

#22 The Secret of Cacklefur Castle

A Christmas Tale

#23 Valentine's Day Disaster

#24 Field Trip to Niagara Falls

#25 The Search for Sunken Treasure

#26 The Mummy with No Name

#27 The Christmas Toy Factory

#28 Wedding Crasher

#29 Down and Out Down Under

#30 The Mouse Island Marathon

#31 The Mysterious Cheese Thief

Christmas Catastrophe

#32 Valley of the Giant Skeletons

#33 Geronimo and the Gold Medal Mystery

#34 Geronimo Stilton, Secret Agent

#35 A Very Merry Christmas

#36 Geronimo's Valentine

#37 The Race Across America

#38 A Fabumouse School Adventure

#39 Singing Sensation

#40 The Karate Mouse

#41 Mighty Mount Kilimanjaro

#42 The Peculiar Pumpkin Thief

#43 I'm Not a Supermouse!

#44 The Giant Diamond Robbery

#45 Save the White Whale!

#46 The Haunted Castle

#47 Run for the Hills, Geronimo!

#48 The Mystery in Venice

#49 The Way of the Samurai

#50 This Hotel Is Haunted!

#51 The Enormouse Pearl Heist

#52 Mouse in Space!

#53 Rumble in the Jungle

#54 Get into Gear, Stilton!

#55 The Golden Statue Plot

#56 Flight of the Red Bandit

The Hunt for the Golden Book

#57 The Stinky Cheese Vacation

#58 The Super Chef Contest

#59 Welcome to Moldy Manor

The Hunt for the Curious Cheese

#60 The Treasure of Easter Island

#61 Mouse House Hunter

#62 Mouse Overboard!

Join me and my friends as we travel through time in these very special editions!

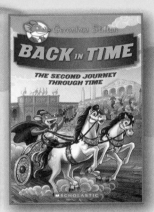

THE JOURNEY THROUGH TIME

BACK IN TIME:
THE SECOND JOURNEY THROUGH TIME

THE RACE AGAINST TIME:
THE THIRD JOURNEY THROUGH TIME

Don't miss any of these exciting Thea Sisters adventures!

Thea Stilton and the
Dragon's Code

Thea Stilton and the
Mountain of Fire

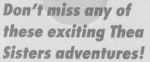

Thea Stilton and the
Ghost of the Shipwreck

Thea Stilton and the
Secret City

Thea Stilton and the
Mystery in Paris

Thea Stilton and the
Cherry Blossom Adventure

Thea Stilton and the
Star Castaways

Thea Stilton: Big Trouble
in the Big Apple

Thea Stilton and the
Ice Treasure

Thea Stilton and the
Secret of the Old Castle

Thea Stilton and the
Blue Scarab Hunt

Thea Stilton and the
Prince's Emerald

Thea Stilton and the Mystery
on the Orient Express

Thea Stilton and the
Dancing Shadows

Thea Stilton and the
Legend of the Fire Flowers

Thea Stilton and the
Spanish Dance Mission

Thea Stilton and the
Journey to the Lion's Den

Thea Stilton and the
Great Tulip Heist

Thea Stilton and the
Chocolate Sabotage

Thea Stilton and the
Missing Myth

Thea Stilton and the
Lost Letters

Thea Stilton and the
Tropical Treasure

Meet
GERONIMO STILTONOOT

He is a cavemouse — Geronimo Stilton's ancient ancestor! He runs the stone newspaper in the prehistoric village of Old Mouse City. From dealing with dinosaurs to dodging meteorites, his life in the Stone Age is full of adventure!

#1 The Stone of Fire

#2 Watch Your Tail!

#3 Help, I'm in Hot Lava!

#4 The Fast and the Frozen

#5 The Great Mouse Race

#6 Don't Wake the Dinosaur!

#7 I'm a Scaredy-Mouse!

#8 Surfing for Secrets

#9 Get the Scoop, Geronimo!

#10 My Autosaurus Will Win!

Be sure to read all of our magical special edition adventures!

THE KINGDOM OF FANTASY

THE QUEST FOR PARADISE:
THE RETURN TO THE KINGDOM OF FANTASY

THE AMAZING VOYAGE:
THE THIRD ADVENTURE IN THE KINGDOM OF FANTASY

THE DRAGON PROPHECY:
THE FOURTH ADVENTURE IN THE KINGDOM OF FANTASY

THE VOLCANO OF FIRE:
THE FIFTH ADVENTURE IN THE KINGDOM OF FANTASY

THE SEARCH FOR TREASURE:
THE SIXTH ADVENTURE IN THE KINGDOM OF FANTASY

THE ENCHANTED CHARMS:
THE SEVENTH ADVENTURE IN THE KINGDOM OF FANTASY

THE PHOENIX OF DESTINY:
AN EPIC KINGDOM OF FANTASY ADVENTURE

THEA STILTON: THE JOURNEY TO ATLANTIS

THEA STILTON: THE SECRET OF THE FAIRIES

THEA STILTON: THE SECRET OF THE SNOW

THEA STILTON: THE CLOUD CASTLE

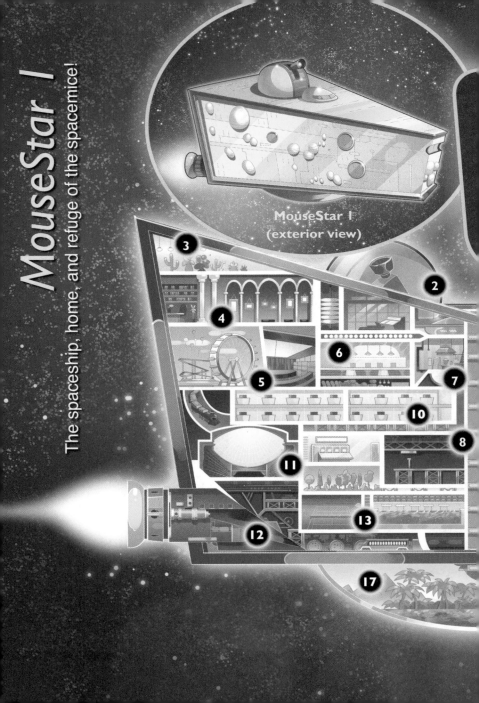

MouseStar 1

The spaceship, home, and refuge of the spacemice!

MouseStar 1
(exterior view)

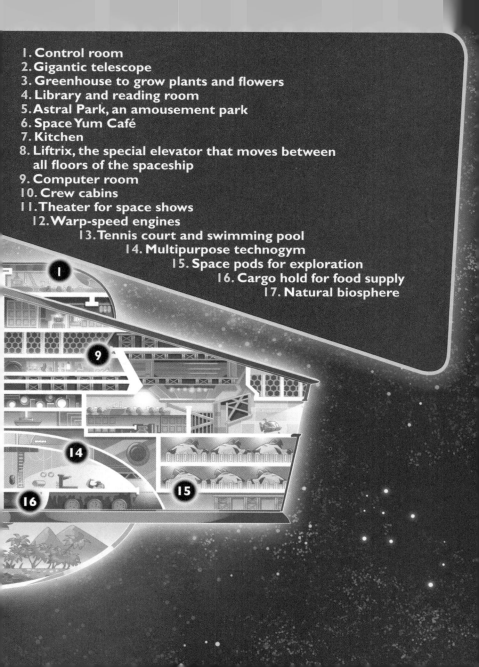

1. Control room
2. Gigantic telescope
3. Greenhouse to grow plants and flowers
4. Library and reading room
5. Astral Park, an amousement park
6. Space Yum Café
7. Kitchen
8. Liftrix, the special elevator that moves between all floors of the spaceship
9. Computer room
10. Crew cabins
11. Theater for space shows
12. Warp-speed engines
13. Tennis court and swimming pool
14. Multipurpose technogym
15. Space pods for exploration
16. Cargo hold for food supply
17. Natural biosphere

Dear mouse friends,
thanks for reading,
and good-bye until the next book.
See you in outer space!

My dear mouse friends,

Have I ever told you how much I love science fiction? I've always wanted to write incredible adventures set in another dimension, but I've never believed that parallel universes exist . . . until now!

That's because my good friend Professor Paws von Volt, the brilliant, secretive scientist, has just made an incredible discovery. Thanks to some mousetropic calculations, he determined that there are many different dimensions in time and space, where anything could be possible.

The professor's work inspired me to write this science fiction adventure in which my family and I travel through space in search of new worlds. We're a fabumouse crew: the spacemice!

I hope you enjoy this intergalactic adventure!

Geronimo Stilton

PROFESSOR PAWS VON VOLT

THE SPACEMICE

GERONIMO
STILTONIX

TRAP
STILTONIX

THEA
STILTONIX

GRANDFATHER
WILLIAM STILTONIX

ROBOTIX

BENJAMIN
STILTONIX
AND BUGSY
WUGSY

Geronimo Stilton

SPACEMICE

BEWARE!
SPACE JUNK!

Scholastic Inc.

Copyright © 2015 by Edizioni Piemme S.p.A., Palazzo Mondadori, Via Mondadori 1, 20090 Segrate, Italy. International Rights © Atlantyca S.p.A. English translation © 2016 by Atlantyca S.p.A.

The publisher does not have any control over and does not assume any responsibility for author or third-party websites or their content.

GERONIMO STILTON names, characters, and related indicia are copyright, trademark, and exclusive license of Atlantyca S.p.A. All rights reserved. The moral right of the author has been asserted. Based on an original idea by Elisabetta Dami. www.geronimostilton.com

Published by Scholastic Inc., *Publishers since 1920,* 557 Broadway, New York, NY 10012. SCHOLASTIC and associated logos are trademarks and/or registered trademarks of Scholastic Inc.

Stilton is the name of a famous English cheese. It is a registered trademark of the Stilton Cheese Makers' Association. For more information, go to www.stiltoncheese.com.

No part of this publication may be reproduced, stored in a retrieval system, or transmitted in any form or by any means, electronic, mechanical, photocopying, recording, or otherwise, without written permission of the copyright holder. For information regarding permission, please contact: Atlantyca S.p.A., Via Leopardi 8, 20123 Milan, Italy; e-mail foreignrights@atlantyca.it, www.atlantyca.com.

This book is a work of fiction. Names, characters, places, and incidents are either the product of the author's imagination or are used fictitiously, and any resemblance to actual persons, living or dead, business establishments, events, or locales is entirely coincidental.

ISBN 978-0-545-87245-4

Text by Geronimo Stilton
Original title *Pericolo spazzatura spaziale!*
Cover by Flavio Ferron
Illustrations by Giuseppe Facciotto (design) and Daniele Verzini (color)
Graphics by Francesca Sirianni

Special thanks to AnnMarie Anderson
Translated by Julia Heim
Interior design by Kevin Callahan / BNGO Books

10 9 8 7 6 5 4 3 2 1   16 17 18 19 20

Printed in the U.S.A.   40

First printing 2016

In the darkness of the farthest galaxy in time and space is a spaceship inhabited exclusively by mice.

This fabumouse vessel is called the **MouseStar 1**, and I am its captain!

I am Geronimo Stiltonix, a somewhat accident-prone mouse who (to tell you the truth) would rather be writing novels than steering a spaceship.

But for now, my adventurous family and I are busy traveling around the universe on exciting intergalactic missions.

THIS IS THE LATEST ADVENTURE OF THE SPACEMICE!

AN ANNUAL INSPECTION

It was a calm Monday on the spaceship *MouseStar 1*. There were no COSMIC disturbances, no alien invasions in the galaxy, and no UNKNOWN planets on the horizon.

Basically, it was a stress-free day, which hadn't happened in **weeks**, MONTHS, or maybe even years! I was about to sit back in my command chair, kick up my paws, and put the spaceship on autopilot.

Then suddenly . . .

BEEP! BEEEEP! BEEEEEEP!

What was that annoying noise?

I looked at the screen in front of me. My

DIGITAL CALENDAR had an urgent meeting on it. Galactic Gorgonzola, I had completely **forgotten**!

Oh, excuse me, I haven't introduced myself: My name is Stiltonix, Geronimo Stiltonix. I'm the captain of the *MouseStar 1*, the most fabumouse spaceship in the universe (though to be honest, my real dream is to be a writer!). Now, where was I? Oh, yes: According to my digital calendar, today was the *MouseStar 1*'s annual MECHANICAL inspection.

I was scheduled to tour the ship with our mechanic, Sally de Wrench. We would closely **examine** the motor room, the boiler room, the garbage storage room, and a *zillion* other places.

Stellar Swiss! I was so nervous about the inspection that my fur was soaked with sweat. You probably think I was **afraid** the ship wouldn't pass the tests! But the real reason for my anxiety was Sally de Wrench. You see, she is the most fascinating mouse in the entire galaxy, and I have an E N O R M O U S E crush on her! Every time I see her, my legs go as soft as cream cheese, my squeak gets stuck in my throat, and my brain turns to Brie!

As I was thinking about Sally, *MouseStar 1*'s onboard computer, Hologramix, spoke up.

"Sally de Wrench is waiting for you on the lower level!"

I began to *TREMBLE* from the ends of

Um . . .

my whiskers to the tip of my tail. I tried to get out of my command chair, but my paws were heavier than wheels of aged Parmesan and my knees **WOBBLED** like sticks of string cheese.

Gulp . . .

Unfortunately, my cousin Trap was sitting next to me, **playing** space checkers against his computer.

Ack!

"What's up, Cuz?" he asked. "You seem **stuck**!"

"N-no, it's nothing,"

5

I stammered, my snout turning red with embarrassment. "I was just getting up."

Trap took one look at me and **figured out** what was going on.

"Looks like someone is afraid to be alone with Sally, hmm?" he teased me.

Come on, Cousin!

Sweet As Honey
on Cheese!

Trap PUSHED me toward the door of the command center.

"Cousin, you are as **sweet** on Sally as honey on cheese," he said, shaking his snout. "But luckily I'm here to help you. Let's go—you don't want to keep her waiting!"

Mousy meteorites! Trap wanted to come with me for the inspection. I knew he would only make me feel even more **embarrassed**! But before I could protest, my cousin had grabbed me by the paw and pushed me into the liftrix, the special elevator that transports spacemice

from one floor of our spaceship to another.

As soon as I stepped into the liftrix, a jet of air whisked me down to the lower levels of the *MouseStar 1*.

"Ahhhh!" I squeaked, caught off guard.

In one galactic second, I **tumbled** out of the glass tube and onto the floor of the lower level of the spaceship. I was about to get up, when . . .

BAM!

Trap **crashed** into me like an out-of-orbit meteorite!

Ha, ha, ha!

Aaaah!

"**Whoops**," my cousin squeaked. "Sorry, Geronimo!"

Before I could GET OUT from under him, I heard a sweet **female** voice.

"Are you okay, **CAPTAIN**?" the voice asked. "What happened?"

Sally de Wrench was right in front of me.

Captain?

Uh . . .

Holey moon craters! How embarrassing!

I got to my paws and tried to think of something *intelligent* to say. But as I stood there staring at Sally's big blue eyes, my thoughts vanished like cheese in a black hole!

Luckily, Trap came to my rescue.

"A pressure problem inside the liftrix made us lose our BALANCE!" he fibbed.

Are you ready, Captain?

"Oh, my," Sally replied. "I'll be sure to take a look at that later. Now, are you ready to begin our **inspection**, Captain?"

"N-no," I stuttered. "I mean, y-yes!"

Trap **pinched** me on the tail. YIKES! I had to get my nerves under control!

I cleared my throat and did my best to sound **confident**.

"Yes, I'm ready!"

Trap patted me on the shoulder so **hard** I almost fell over again.

"Good," he said with a wink. "I'll head back to the **COMMAND CENTER**, then. See you later, Cuz!"

And so I **set out** on my inspection of the *MouseStar 1* with Sally as my guide. She explained all the **TECHNICAL** details to me as we toured the spaceship. Even though I'm the captain, I have to admit that I don't have a **CLUE** about how the ship works! It's a good thing Sally is such an **excellent** mechanic.

"Well, that's **everything**, Captain!" Sally announced after we had completed our inspection of the craft's **air filters**.

I tried to think of something witty to squeak so that I'd get just a little more time with Sally, but my mind went completely BLANK.

"Um, er, e-e-everything seems to be okay!" I stuttered.

Sally smiled.

"If you need any further explanations, just let me know," she said kindly.

Then she shook my paw and walked off.

The touch of her paw made me turn redder than the planet Mars. Oh, I'm such a hopeless romantic!

DON'T BE LATE!

As soon as I returned to the **command center**, Trap practically jumped on my tail.

"So, how did it go?" he asked.

"Well, Sally did SHAKE my paw," I said with a sigh. "But I couldn't think of anything intelligent to say!"

"When's the next inspection?" Trap asked.

"Not for another six months," I replied.

"But that's such a LONG time from now!" my cousin said with a gasp.

"That's the protocol," I said with a shrug. "And I'll have plenty of time to write my novel in the meantime."

Trap shook his head. Then he got a mischievous gleam in his eye. That look meant only one thing: trouble!

"Wh-what is it?" I asked, suddenly very worried. My cousin always seems to come up with the most IMPOSSIBLE schemes!

"Geronimo, what do you say we have a nice dinner together tonight?" he asked INNOCENTLY.

"Thanks, but I'm very busy —" I began.

"Come on!" he said, cutting me off. "We can have a FONDUE FEAST! We never spend any quality time together."

Hmm. I considered his proposal. The *MouseStar 1*'s chef, Squizzy, does make delicious fondue.

"Oh, all right," I said. "You convinced me! After all, it's easier to write on a full stomach."

"Meet me at eight at the Space Yum Café," Trap ordered. "And don't be late!"

I headed back to my room to get ready. As soon as I opened the door, my personal assistant robot, **ASSISTATRIX**, grabbed me, lifted me up, and dropped me in my *SparkleMousix* shower pod.

"**HELP!**" I squeaked. "Let me go!"

But Assistatrix **ignored** me. A moment later, my fur was being scrubbed, rinsed, and dried.

Then it was time to get **dressed**.

"Captain, I suggest you wear a *dinner jacket* and your *tie* with the galaxies on it," Assistatrix said.

"Dinner jacket?!" I protested. "But I'm not going to an interstellar gala!"

"Your cousin **advised**

First the SparkleMousix . . .

then the clothes . . .

and, finally, the cologne!

me to dress you **elegantly**!" Assistatrix said.

"But you're *my* personal assistant robot, not Trap's," I replied. "You're supposed to do what I —"

Before I could finish my sentence, though, Assistatrix had slipped the suit over my head and sprayed me in a cloud of COSMIC CHEDDAR COLOGNE!

Then it nudged me out of my room with a firm **shove**.

"Hurry, Captain," it yelled. "You're already late!"

I looked around, hoping to catch an astrotaxi to the Space Yum Café.

Then I heard a little voice behind me. "**UNCLE G!** You look so elegant!"

It was my sweet nephew Benjamin and his friend Bugsy Wugsy!

"Hi!" I greeted them. "I'm meeting Trap for dinner."

The mouselets began to giggle. It was almost as if they knew something I didn't.

"Yes, he told us!" Bugsy squeaked.

"Actually, could you bring him these?" Benjamin added,

handing me a box of Gorgonzola chocolates.

"But why?" I asked, confused.

"Um, he forgot them in the command room," Bugsy explained.

"**Hurry**, Uncle," Benjamin squeaked. "You don't want to make, um, *Trap* wait!"

Bugsy Wugsy and Benjamin burst into giggles again. What was so funny?

When I arrived at the Space Yum Café, Squizzy greeted me at the entrance. "Welcome, **Captain**!" he said. "Your cousin Trap told me to inform you that he will arrive in a moment. Meanwhile, please come this way!"

Squizzy led me to a private room in the back of the restaurant. A giant WiNDOW offered a breathtaking view of the galaxy.

"Are you sure this is our table?" I asked, stunned. It seemed a little too FANCY for a quick bite with Trap.

"Of course, Captain!" Squizzy answered, **lighting** a candle on the table.

Stellar Swiss! A candle? What was going on?

A DATE IN SPACE!

A moment later, I heard a sound. I turned to see . . . Sally de Wrench!

My paws began to sweat and my tail twisted into a knot. She looked extraordinary! Her long evening gown *SHIMMERED* in the galaxy light, and her eyes **sparkled** like stars.

But just a minute! What was she doing here?!

We LOOKED at each other in silence for a second. Then we both squeaked at once:

"But . . . where's Trap?"

"But . . . where's Thea?"

But . . . where's Thea?

Then I understood: My **SNEAKY** cousin Trap had led me to believe we were going to dinner together. But he had arranged for me to have dinner with **Sally** instead. That's why I was so dᴘessed up!

And my sister, Thea, must have done the same thing to **SALLY**!

But . . . where's Trap?

"So that's why Thea insisted I look elegant," Sally said as she sat down at the table with me.

And that's why Benjamin had given me the Gorgonzola chocolates: It was a **present** for Sally! With my heart pounding, I handed her the box.

"A s-small gift for you," I stuttered.

She smiled at me, and I turned **BRiGHt RED**!

"Thank you!" she said. "You're quite a **gentlemouse**, Captain!"

I melted like fondue when I heard the compliment.

"This is a really beautiful view, isn't it?" I asked, trying to keep my whiskers from SHAKING as I squeaked.

"Yes," Sally agreed, smiling **kindly**. "Trap and Thea certainly went out of their way to organize a really **mouserific** evening for us!"

A moment later, *Squizzy* arrived with our menus.

Onion soup WITH FRENCH BREAD AND MELTED GALAXY GRUYÈRE ON TOP

Fried Parmesan wedge WITH A MARTIAN-SPACEBERRY-FONDUE DIPPING SAUCE

Intergalactic salad WITH FOUR CHEESES

Moon-mozzarella-flavored ice cream sundae

SPLATTT!

After a few moments of awkward silence, Sally got the conversation going.

"So, what do you like to do best, Captain?" she asked.

"Er—well, to tell you the truth, my real passion is *writing*," I admitted.

"Wow!" Sally exclaimed. "I had no idea. What are you working on?"

"It's a NOVEL called —"

But before I could finish my sentence . . .

Something **slimy** and **sludgy** splattered against the window of the dining room! I decided to ignore it. I wouldn't let that goopy slime interfere with my romantic dinner!

"As I was saying," I continued. "I'm writing a novel about spacemice. I'm still on the first chapter—"

Ding! Splash! Glop!

Sally and I turned toward the window. Hundreds of objects in all shapes and sizes were speeding straight toward the *MouseStar 1*!

A moment later, Hologramix **appeared** in the air in front of us.

"YELLOW ALERT! YELLOW ALERT! YELLOW ALERT!" Hologramix shouted.

Martian mozzarella! A yellow alert? That meant there was a real emergency. We were in danger!

"Our spaceship is passing through a galaxy cluster of unidentified objects,"

Hologramix explained. "Captain, get to the control room right away!"

How unlucky! A yellow alert right in the middle of my dinner with Sally!

"I'm sorry, Sally," I said with a sigh. "But I really have to go."

"Don't worry, Captain," she replied quickly. "I'm happy to come with you! I'll help you figure out what those objects are."

We hopped in an astrotaxi and ZOOMED toward the command center. When we stepped into the room, everyone turned to look at us.

Trap and Thea winked at me, Benjamin and Bugsy Wugsy giggled under their whiskers, and Grandfather William looked

ANGRIER than a cosmocat with space fleas!

"What took you so long, Grandson?" my grandfather grumbled. "And look how you're dressed. Don't tell me that you were at a fancy gala while our spaceship is splashing through a sea of space junk!"

"Um, hello, Grandfather!" I replied, not sure what else I should say.

"Why aren't you ever at your post when

there's an EMERGENCY?" he continued to berate me.

"Don't be **angry**, sir," Sally intervened. "Your grandson was at dinner with me."

Suddenly, my grandfather changed his attitude.

"Oh, excuse me!" he replied. "Well, everyone deserves a night off every now and then, right?"

Incredible! Sally had managed to defend me successfully to my grandfather!

"Of course," Sally agreed. "Now, let's get to more important issues: Did you say something earlier about SPACE JUNK?"

"Yes!" Grandfather replied. "Space junk is *HITTING* us at top speeds!"

WATCH OUT:
JUNK AHEAD!

Space junk? What was my grandfather talking about?

"Space junk is a conglomeration of many unwanted objects that are floating through space," explained Professor Greenfur, *MouseStar 1*'s resident scientist.

To be precise . . .

Sally **NODDED** in agreement and squeaked, "I think I saw a piece of an old motor!"

But **Robotix**, the ship's know-it-all multipurpose robot, corrected her.

"To be precise, it was a piece of an **iNTerStellaR waVe** antenna," he said.

"Are we in danger?" I asked. I was **worried** about my ship and its crew.

"Not if we remain ꓢTILL," Thea explained. "That's why I already turned off the motors. But if we start up the ship again, a piece of metal could **DAMAGE** the external hull!"

It could take weeks!

"Well, what do we do **now**?" Trap asked impatiently. "Wait until the junk floats away?"

"Yes, but that could take days, or even weeks!" **Professor Greenfur** replied.

Solar smoked Gouda! We had to come up with another solution.

Suddenly, I remembered something I'd seen during the inspection that morning.

"We could collect the garbage and recycle it using the Stellar Garbage Sortrix," I suggested.

"That's a great idea!" Benjamin exclaimed. "We learned all about recycling in school.

From the Encyclopedia Galactica

STELLAR GARBAGE SORTRIX

A superstellar piece of machinery that can analyze, break down, and recycle garbage and waste. The Stellar Garbage Sortrix then uses the recycled materials to create small objects for use in daily life.

Instead of **THROWING** all the garbage out, the Sortrix will divide it up based on the material it's made of. Then it can be broken down and turned into **new objects**."

Professor Greenfur did some calculations. "We should be able to clean everything up and get *moving* again in about three galactic hours!"

Everyone cheered.

"Well done, Grandson," my grandfather said, a look of surprise on his snout. "I knew there was a reason I appointed you captain of this spaceship!"

I couldn't believe it. Was Grandfather really complimenting me? That only happened once in a **blue-cheese** moon.

"Um, wow! Thanks," I replied, still stunned.

But then Grandfather continued. "Since

you had such a great idea, Geronimo, I elect you to be the official space junk collector!"

Ah, I knew it was too good to be true!

"Come on, Cuz," Trap said confidently. "I'll come with you! A bit of **exercise** will be good for us!"

"But I suffer from terrible space sickness whenever I go on a space walk!" I squeaked in **protest**.

"Aw, you'll be fine," Trap replied.

There was nothing I could do. A few moments later, I was wearing a spacesuit and headed off into the cosmos to pick up the trash!

Soon I heard Sally's voice through a microphone in my helmet.

"When you're ready, I'll activate the vacuum," she explained. "You'll use it to

SUCK UP all the space junk."

"Ready!" Trap squeaked immediately.

I was still trying to figure out how my spacesuit worked, but it was **too late**.

The vacuum was already on, and the tube had wrapped itself around me!

"Grab the handle, Geronimo!" Trap yelled.

HaNdle? I reached out and tried to AIM the tube toward a mass of garbage. But my paw ended up at the mouth of the tube instead, and I was nearly sucked inside.

"Trap, heeeeeelp!" I squeaked in **terror**.

Luckily, he quickly came to my rescue.

Then a piece of trash got stuck in the tube and Sally had to reverse the flow to get it out. But I didn't move in time — and I was blasted with a spray of liquid garbage.

Mousey meteorites, what a day!

WHOSE TRASH IS IT?

Once we had successfully vacuumed up all the trash, Trap and I RE**T**URNED to the command center.

"Great work, team!" Thea cheered. Then she turned the *MouseStar 1*'s motors back on and we began moving again.

"I wonder where all that trash came from," Professor Greenfur mused.

"Well, if you had ever thought to ask your resident robot genius for help, you might know the answer," Robotix replied in a very ANNOYED tone. "But no. Instead you rely on that digital fur-faced illusion that appears and disappears whenever it wants!"

Sure enough, in an instant, Hologramix **appeared**.

"How dare you!" the computer countered. "I resolve seven hundred forty-nine queries every second!"

How dare you!

Fur-faced illusion!

"And yet you don't know how to identify a simple piece of garbage!" Robotix replied in a huff.

Somehow, Trap managed to calm the two of them. They never missed a chance to fight about which one was a more developed form of **artificial intelligence**.

Once they had stopped arguing, I took Robotix's bait.

"Robotix, do you know where the space

junk came from?" I asked.

The robot looked at me with **satisfaction**.

"Of course!" he replied. "The trash is from Planet Cleanix, Captain! It's easy to figure it out: Just look at the pieces of metal out there."

"Huh?" I asked, confused. Robotix just sighed and shook his head.

"My memory bank contains a list of all the robotics that have ever been produced in this GaLaXY," Robotix explained. "And these pieces come from Cleanix!"

"So all the trash must be from Cleanix," Trap concluded. "stellar swiss, what littermice!"

"It's true," Professor Greenfur confirmed a moment later. "I calculated the *trajectory* of the garbage, and the planet Cleanix is located right in this part of the galaxy, so it all makes sense!"

"Okay, we now know Cleanix has a garbage-disposal problem," I said with a yawn. "Now if you'll excuse me, I really need to get some sleep. It's very late and I'm so tired. And tomorrow —"

"Tomorrow we head to **Cleanix**!" Grandfather William interrupted. "This galaxy belongs to all of us, and everyone must work together to keep it CLEAN."

"Of course," I agreed. "But we already cleaned up the mess ourselves."

"That doesn't matter!" Grandfather explained. "It is our DUTY to understand what's happening there. Maybe they could use our hELP. Isn't that right, Captain?"

"Y-yes, of course," I said quickly.

Sally agreed as well.

"It's true," she said. "That floating garbage

could be really DANGEROUS for other spaceships! We need to do something about it right away."

Next stop: the planet Cleanix!

Our **mission** was clear.

"Spacemice, tomorrow morning, we leave for **Cleanix**!"

SPARKLY CLEAN SPARKLINA

At seven the next morning, the whole *MouseStar 1* crew was in the command center and ready to *go*.

I cleared my throat.

"Thea, are all systems ready?"

"Yes, Captain!" my sister replied.

"Then let's head toward Cleanix at supersonic speed!" I ordered.

When we neared the planet, Thea slowed down the ship so that she could maneuver around large *heaps* of garbage that were floating in space.

Suddenly, Benjamin pointed at something outside the spaceship.

"Look, Uncle!" he squeaked. "You can see Cleanix. Doesn't it look ODD?"

I peeked out the enormouse command center window. Sure enough, the planet was straight ahead of us. Half of it was unusually bright and sparkly, while the other half was wrapped in a GREENISH FOG.

"How strange!" I agreed. "Hologramix, what do you know about this planet and its inhabitants?"

The computer responded instantly: "Half the planet is populated by Cleanix aliens, while the other half is uninhabited. Cleanix aliens are known for their excellent manners and extreme cleanliness."

I breathed a **Sigh** of relief. Maybe we would finally have a **peaceful** mission!

"We have reached the safety distance from the planet," Thea announced. "The landing ship is **PREPARED**, and I've alerted the Cleanix aliens to our arrival."

"Great work!" I exclaimed. "Trap and Thea, put on your spacesuits and get ready for our **MISSION**!"

I felt a tug at my sleeve, and I looked down into the **wide** eyes of my sweet nephew.

"Uncle, can we come, too?" he asked. "We learned all about the capital of Cleanix in school. **Sparklina** is a very high-tech city, and we would really love to see it!"

I looked at Benjamin and Bugsy. They were so excited! And it did seem like it would be a pretty safe excursion.

"Okay," I replied. "But you have to

promise you'll stay near us the entire time. Agreed?"

"**of course, uncle G!**" they replied in unison.

"Then I guess we're all ready to —"

I was interrupted by a **METALLIC** voice:

"Captain, you aren't forgetting about me, are you?"

I turned to see Robotix glaring at me as **smoke** billowed out of his air vents. **Galactic Gorgonzola!** He was furious.

"I'm the one who told you where the trash was coming from," he reminded me. "So I **insist** that I come on this mission!"

"Um, yes, of course, Robotix," I reassured him. "You'll come, too!"

So we all boarded the space pod, our small landing ship, and headed for Sparklina!

How Embarrassing!

Sparklina was a truly **FANTASTIC** city. There were tall, shiny towers; superclean streets; and large, colorful signs everywhere. Everything shimmered. Honestly, it was all a bit much for my taste. I wished I had remembered to wear my **sunglasses**!

We flew over the city and then headed to the spaceport. A delegation of Cleanix aliens were waiting there to meet us. They had put out a velvet carpet for us, and there was a FLOATING table filled with delectable **space treats**!

As soon as we landed, a tall, elegantly dressed alien approached us. He smelled strongly of my *favorite* cologne: Cheesy Moon Craters No. 5.

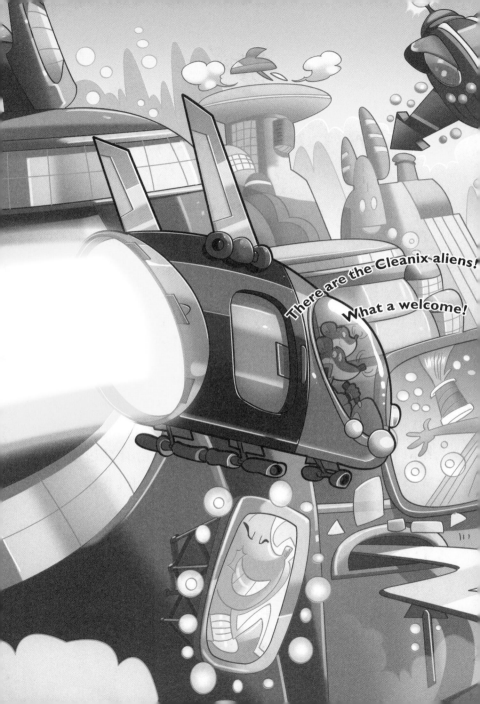

"I am the emperor, **Samuel Sparkle**," he introduced himself. "Welcome to Cleanix, dear friends!"

I was a bit **embarrassed** by all the splendor, but I tried to assume a tone that was appropriate for the occasion.

"We spacemice are pleased to meet you," I replied. "Thank you for the warm welcome! I am Geronimo Stiltonix, the captain of

Welcome!

Pleased to meet you!

the *MouseStar 1*."

"Psst, Geronimo!" Trap whispered in my ear. "While you're handling the pleasantries, we're going to go **nibble** on some snacks, okay?"

I didn't have a chance to respond because my cousin was already **dashing** toward the table and snatching up whatever his paws could reach.

Yum!

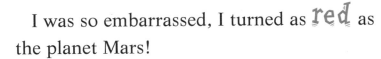

I was so embarrassed, I turned as red as the planet Mars!

"Umm . . . y-you must, er, excuse them," I explained sheepishly. "It's been a long trip."

The emperor smiled. "No problem!" he replied. "But tell me, what brings you here?"

Thea stepped forward. "During our galactic travels, we drove right into a stream of GARBAGE that almost damaged our spaceship," she explained. "The garbage seemed to be coming from your planet. Do you know anything about this?"

The emperor lost his sparkling smile immediately.

"I don't know what you're talking about," he replied dryly. "Sparklina is the cleanest and most orderly city in the entire galaxy!"

BLACK HOLEY GALAXIES! We had

irritated him. I tried to be a bit more diplomatic than Thea had been.

"Please excuse us," I explained. "We didn't mean to question your **cleanliness**! We're just trying to understand where the garbage is coming from."

The emperor's ꜱᴏᴜʀ expression didn't change.

"Um, when we arrived, we also noticed that half your planet is surrounded by a greenish fog," I pointed out, trying again. "Is everything okay on Cleanix?"

"That half is uninhabitable!" **Emperor Sparkle** replied quickly. "Don't worry about it! Now, my daughter, SHIMMER, will show you around our city."

At that moment, a very elegant alien stepped forward. Even Trap stopped *snacking* for a moment to say hello.

"It would be an *honor* to show you around our fair city," Shimmer said smoothly. "Please FOLLOW me and we can start the tour right away!"

"We're coming," my cousin Trap replied quickly, his snout **stuffed** with food. How rude!

But Shimmer wasn't insulted. Instead, she looked **amused**!

"Farewell, spacemice," the emperor said. "I will be happy to meet with you again after your tour. **But one bit of advice:** Don't waste your time thinking about garbage. Why don't you concentrate on shopping for some NEW SPACESUITS? You could use them!"

I looked at my spacesuit, **confused**. Sure,

it was a little bit worn, but it was still totally functional. Plus I really liked it!

Meanwhile, at the emperor's signal, a ROBOT had immediately started vacuuming up the dirt on the carpet—and all the leftover food on the table!

"Uncle, they threw **everything** away!" Benjamin exclaimed in surprise.

What a waste!

WHOOOOOOSH

What a waste!

Supershiny, Supersparkly, Superclean!

The tour of Sparklina began on a long street that crossed the whole city. It was decorated with all kinds of **monuments**.

"Farther down this street you can admire the statue of my grandfather, Reginald Shiny," Shimmer told us.

As I studied the sparkly statue—which was decorated with DIAMONDS and other precious stones—I thought I saw a small, very DIRTY, and very **rusty** robot dart around a corner.

GALACTIC GORGONZOLA! How was that possible? Everything on Cleanix seemed to be brand-new.

I was about to follow the robot when Trap distracted me.

"G, I can't take it anymore!" he whined. "These statues are so **boring**. They're all the same!"

"**Sshhh!**" I whispered under my whiskers. "Have a little more *patience . . .*"

Unfortunately, Shimmer had heard him, but strangely, she didn't get mad. She actually started to *laugh*!

"Trap is right. That's enough of these boring statues!" she said. "I just had an idea: I'll take you to a place that's much more **fun**!"

"Sounds great!" Trap cheered.

A few minutes later, we found ourselves in front of a **supertall**, **supershiny**, **SUPERSPARKLY**, and obviously **superclean** building!

Shimmer led us to the entrance.

"Welcome to the Cosmic Mega Mall," she said proudly. "It's the *largest* shopping mall in the universe. You can find products from every corner of the galaxy."

Martian mozzarella! That place wasn't just big—it was *immense*!

There were luxury stores everywhere. Extremely elegant Cleanix aliens were coming and going, their bags filled with clothes, food, and objects of all kinds.

"But what are they going to do with all this STUFF?" Trap asked, stunned.

"The Cleanix people like constantly changing our clothes, furniture, computers, and spaceships," she explained. "We love everything new!"

"But what do you do with the old objects?"

"We throw them away," Shimmer replied simply. "We aren't INTERESTED in things once they are used."

As Shimmer spoke, I watched an alien leaving one store with tons of bags. She stopped to take off her jacket—and she threw it into a floating trash can, and then put on a new jacket she had just bought!

Only then did I **notice** that the shopping mall was full of floating trash cans and garbage robots that were gathering everything the Cleanix aliens were throwing away.

I was pretty sure I had an idea where all that **trash** ended up. But when I turned to ask Shimmer, she was dragging Trap toward a custom-made clothing boutique.

"You'll look so great in something COLORFUL and NEW!" Shimmer told my cousin.

Meanwhile, Benjamin and Bugsy Wugsy had spotted a VIDEO GAME store.

"See you later, Uncle G!" they called with a wave as they raced toward it.

I looked around for Thea and saw her entering a gigantic vehicle shop to look at the latest spaceship models.

It seemed as if everyone had abandoned me. Even Robotix was in a robot accessories store! I could see him **ARGUING** with a shop clerk about something.

I was on my own. *What should I do?* I thought. I looked at the hologram **map** of the mall. My eyes lit up when I saw that there was a bookstore on the seventh floor. **Mousy meteorites!** I had to get there right away!

SOMETHING STINKS . . .

I went **UP** a series of escalators floor by floor (luckily there was no liftrix on Cleanix!). I was almost at the seventh floor when, through a **shopwindow**, I noticed something flying around outside.

As I wondered what it was . . .

BANG!

I found myself lying on the floor in pain. While I had been busy looking out the window, the escalator had come to an **end**!

As I got back to my paws, I spotted a *small*, **dirty**, **RUSTY** robot dart behind a trash can. It was the same one I had seen earlier on the city's main street!

The robot tried to zoom away, but I quickly **grabbed** him.

"Who are you?" I asked. "You're different from the other robots around here."

The robot looked around suspiciously.

"I'm a spy!" he said. "I'm **following you** to figure out if you're a friend or an enemy!"

"Enemy?" I asked NERVOUSLY. "Whose enemy?"

"You might be an enemy of the rebel robots who have been thrown away like garbage!" the creature said proudly. "We're preparing

Hey!

for an invasion. We want the Cleanix aliens to understand that they can't just **toss us** aside."

"What do you mean?" I asked, very curious.

"First they sent all the robots they didn't want anymore to the other half of the planet," he explained. "Now they've started launching us into space with their **Galactic Garbage Shooter**!"

"Galactic what?" I asked, perplexed.

"If you go to the **top floor** —"

But before the spy robot could finish his sentence, one of the garbage robots approached.

"**Class Z** robot trash detected," the garbage robot said in a **Metallic** voice. "Vacuum immediately!"

Then he vacuumed up the little robot

before turning to face me.

"Contamination detected!" the robot said. "Begin disinfecting!"

I didn't have time to move a paw before I was covered from ears to tail in white foam. A second later, a stream of **HOT** air dried me off.

"Have a good day, sir!" the robot said when the cleaning was complete.

Disinfecting!

Drying!

Have a good day!

Gulp!

Stinky space cheese, what was that about?

First the dusty little Spy robot, then the garbage robot with his Vacuuming and DiSiNFECTiNG devices . . . something strange was going on!

Suddenly, I remembered what the spy robot had told me before he was vacuumed up:

"If you go to the top floor . . ."

So I went to the top of the building, where I found a panoramic terrace with a beautiful view of the entire city.

Initially, I didn't notice anything strange at all. But then I looked through one of the telescopes mounted around the edge of the roof. What I saw made me jump back in shock. In the distance, an enormouse catapult was shooting mounds of objects

into orbit. It was the **Galactic Garbage Shooter** the spy robot had been taking about!

Black Holey Galaxies! It was true! The Cleanix aliens launched their garbage into space!

I had to return immediately to the others to tell them what I had discovered! When I arrived back on the ground floor, the first one I found was Robotix.

"Captain!" he greeted me. "Look at my NEW antenna! I had to negotiate for a while, but —"

"Yes, yes, that's very nice," I interrupted. "Have you seen the others? It's important!"

At that moment, Thea **popped** out of the store she had been in.

"I'm right here, G!" she called excitedly. "I just bought a supercomfortable space scooter. It's parked right outside . . ."

"Okay, okay," I replied quickly. "But where are Benjamin and Bugsy?"

"Uncle!" squeaked a small voice behind me. "Look what we **WON**!"

The two mouselets showed me a copy of the latest popular **VIDEO GAME**.

"Great," I said. "Now, where's Trap?"

"**HERE I AM**, Cuz!" my cousin shouted. "So, how do I look?"

How do I look?

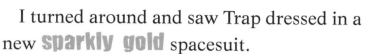

I turned around and saw Trap dressed in a new sparkly gold spacesuit.

"Terrific," I replied. "Do you know where SHIMMER is?"

"Oh, she went to buy some new shoes," Trap explained. "She was wearing a pair she got yesterday, but she thinks the STYLES have changed already."

I was RELIEVED to hear that the emperor's daughter was busy somewhere else. I turned to my friends and lowered my voice. Then I told them about my encounter with the spy robot and about what I had seen from the top floor of the building.

"This story stinks!" Thea exclaimed when I had finished. "And it's not just because it's about garbage! The emperor didn't tell us the TRUTH when we asked. I wonder what else he's hiding!"

AN UNAUTHORIZED EXPEDITION

Thea and I had just made a plan to do some investigating when Shimmer **returned** with four new pairs of shoes. Everyone showed her their purchases.

"I knew you'd **like** it here!" she said, smiling brightly. "No one can resist the allure of the shopping mall! But now we need to return to the imperial palace. My father will be **UPSET** if we're late."

Thea and I exchanged a glance. We had to **slip away**! Suddenly, I had an idea.

"Speaking of your dad, uh, I'm a little **embarrassed** about these clothes," I told Shimmer, gesturing toward my

crumpled spacesuit. "I'd love to buy a new outfit before we head back."

"Of course, Captain!" she quickly agreed. "I didn't want to *offend* you, but that spacesuit you're wearing belongs in the **trash**! Come on, I know a great store —"

"No, no," Thea quickly intervened. "I'll go with him because, uh, I know what he likes!"

"And these two mouselings and I didn't get a chance to stop at the **CANDY** shop," Trap added. "Would you come with us, Shimmer?"

Happy shopping!

"Definitely!" she said. "As long as we don't take too long, we'll get back to the palace **on time**. Let's meet back here in a bit. **HAPPY SHOPPING!**"

As soon as Shimmer was out of sight, Thea and I *headed* toward the spaceport, where our space pod was parked.

Before we could reach our ship, though, an alien from the imperial guard stepped in front of us.

"Hold it right there, spacemice!" the guard ordered. "You cannot use your spaceship without the emperor's authorization."

Hold it right there!

Huh?!

HOLEY SPACE SWISS! Now what?

But Thea was prepared. She put on a friendly smile.

"Won't you please help us?" she asked sweetly. "We just need to run back up to the *MouseStar 1* to get the rest of our crew. This mall is so wonderful, we wanted to give our friends a chance to experience it for themselves."

"I'm sorry, but I cannot let you pass," the guard responded SEVERELY. "Emperor's orders."

"I don't think the emperor would be happy if he knew that you refused friendly guests the right to go shopping," Thea said slyly. "We had heard that the hospitality on Cleanix was the best in the entire universe. But it turns out that's not true. How disappointing!"

The guard looked flustered.

"Oh, well . . . I . . . umm . . ." he mumbled. After a moment of hesitation, he finally stepped aside.

"Go ahead," he said quickly.

We scooted past him immediately, thrilled at our GOOD LUCK.

"Way to go, Thea!" I said as we hopped into the space pod.

Thea immediately pointed our spacecraft toward the part of the planet surrounded by GREEN FOG. We saw black mountains and dark gray clouds on the horizon.

What an UGLY landscape. We were flying over an enormouse garbage dump! Trash was piled up as far as the eye could see. There were scraps of metal, computers, clothes, furniture, robots, spaceships, and more.

"It's so sad," Thea said, shaking her snout. "How could they do this to their planet?"

Suddenly, I noticed some MOVEMENT under one of the heaps of trash.

"Thea, use the ZOOM scope on that patch of garbage!" I said, pointing to the spot below us.

Look!

We were shocked by what appeared on the SCREEN. Hundreds of discarded robots were emerging from the trash!

"What's going on?" Thea asked. "It looks like the trash is coming to life!"

I remembered the spy robot's words: "We're preparing for an invasion . . ."

Galactic Gorgonzola! This wasn't good.

"Thea, I'm afraid these rebel robots are about to invade Sparklina," I said, worried. I quickly reminded her of what the SPY robot had told me back at the shopping mall.

"Oh no!" Thea cried. "The Cleanix aliens haven't treated those discarded robots—or their planet—very well. But there has to be another solution. We need to warn the emperor about their plan to invade Sparklina!"

STOP RIGHT THERE, SPACEMICE!

With our motors at *full speed*, we headed back to Sparklina. But as soon as we got out of our space pod, a member of the imperial guard intercepted us.

"Spacemice, you are **under arrest** by order of the emperor," he said harshly. "You flew your spacecraft over the **PROHIBITED** area!"

"*U-under a-arrest?*" I stuttered. "But we have extremely important information to —"

"Silence!" the guard ordered. "Now follow me to the imperial palace!"

STINKY SPACE CHEESE!

This was just what we needed!

We've been imprisoned!

As we followed the guard, I carefully activated my **wrist communicator** and called Trap.

"Cousin, we've been arrested!" I whispered so the guard couldn't hear. "Where are you?"

He responded immediately.

"We're imprisoned in the emperor's palace," he explained quickly. "He found out that you took the space pod to SNOOP on the other side of the planet, and he came after us!"

"We found a bunch of discarded *rebellious robots*," I told Trap. "We think they're about to invade Sparklina and —"

I was interrupted by sudden **shouts**. I turned and saw some Cleanix aliens running at top speed.

The rebel robots had already entered the city!

In the distance, I saw a **rusted** robot squirting **oil** on buildings. A bit farther off, an old **garbage truck** was pouring its contents out onto the street and sidewalks. Another robot made out of **HOUSEHOLD APPLIANCES** was blaring music that was so loud and **high-pitched**, it was breaking

windows all around us!

Suddenly, a shadow fell over me. I turned and saw an enormouse rebel robot made of MACHINE parts moving toward me threateningly.

Shooting stars! I was in trouble!

A moment before I was crushed by the robot, Thea pulled me out of the way.

I was TREMBLING from the ends of my whiskers to the tip of my tail. I had almost lost my fur!

"Thanks, Thea!" I gasped. "Just one astrosecond later and I would have been as flat as a fur-covered flying saucer!"

"No problem, G!" she said with a wink. "Where did the guard go?"

"He ran," I explained. "He must have been SCARED!"

"Well, that's *good news* for us," Thea

replied. "Let's get to the emperor's palace immediately . . . The rebel robots are heading that way!"

When we reached the palace, though, we realized we were **too late**. The rebel robots had already arrived! The palace entrance was covered in broken glass and metal.

WHAT A GALACTIC MESS!

Oh no!

We're too late!

You're Finally Here, Captain!

Thea and I entered the imperial palace **SLOWLY**, keeping an eye out for the rebel robots. The building was almost completely **DESTROYED**: There was broken glass everywhere, and statues were in pieces.

"It's completely empty," Thea observed. "Where are the Cleanix aliens? And where are our friends?"

At that moment, we heard noises above us. We **climbed** some stairs and found an imperial guard tied up with electrical **cords**.

"What happened?" Thea asked as we freed him.

"Those recycled **ROBOTS** **CAPTURED** the emperor, his wife, and their daughter," the guard explained. "They want to throw them into **space**!"

Oh NO! It sounded like the robots were planning to get their **revenge** on the Cleanix aliens

What happened?

The rebel robots want to take back the city!

for flinging them into space with their Galactic Garbage Shooter.

"The leader of the rebel robots is one of the emperor's old personal-computer robots," the guard explained. "He said he wants to take back the city."

Things were starting to make more **sense**. The recycled robots wanted to live in Sparklina instead of being thrown away and tossed into space!

"Maybe the **SPACEMICE** can help settle the dispute," I told the guard.

"Great idea, Captain," Thea agreed. "But first we need to free our friends."

The guard seemed to **trust** us.

"The other spacemice are locked in the basement," he said. "Follow me!"

We hurried down to a large metal door. The guard punched a code on a keypad, and the door  open. There were our friends!

"It's so good to see you, Uncle!" Benjamin said, giving me a little **PECK** on the snout.

"It's about time!" Trap exclaimed. "I was starting to get a little *hungry*."

"Well, you may still have to wait," I told him. "A lot has been happening!"

"Of course, some of us already know that," Robotix said in an **ANNOYED** tone. "Thanks to my new antenna, I've been **listening in** on the rebel robots' conversations."

"Really?" Thea asked, her ears perking up. "What are they saying?"

"The robots and all the other electronics discarded by the Cleanix aliens have organized," he explained. "They want to prove that they're still **useful**, and that it isn't right to just throw them in the TRASH!"

It was just as I had thought! But there was one thing that I didn't understand.

"I thought I saw a robot made out of **kitchen appliances**," I told Robotix. "Who built it? Did the rebel robots put it together by themselves?"

"Of course!" Robotix said. He sounded insulted. "The Cleanix aliens tossed out very *sophisticated* artisanal robots that were still in working order. And robots are very **INTELLIGENT**, you know!"

"We have to do SOMETHING," Thea said. "There's no time to lose!"

"We need to get to the *Galactic Garbage Shooter* immediately," I agreed. "If the Cleanix aliens and the rebel robots have any chance of working things out, we have to first SAVE the emperor and his family!"

The guard **led us** to the palace garage, where the *SUPERLUXURIOUS* (but supertiny!) imperial spaceship was parked.

"We won't all fit in there!" I squeaked.

Trap **pushed me** inside unceremoniously.

"Stop complaining!" he scolded me. "We just need to **squeeze**!"

Squeak!

Squeeze in!

Ready to Launch!

We **flew** over the city, which was much less **bright** and sparkly since the robot attack.

"There it is!" Benjamin exclaimed when the **Galactic Garbage Shooter** appeared before us.

SOLAR SMOKED GOUDA! Thousands of robots were milling around!

We landed on a small hill and slowly made our way through the robots. They didn't seem to care about us at all. Instead, they were all looking at the Galactic Garbage Shooter.

Unfortunately, the recycled robots were so **TALL**, I wouldn't have been able to see a comet even if it had flown right over my head!

Hmm . . .

Can you see anything?

"Trap, let me climb up on your shoulders," I told my cousin. "That way I can **SEE** what's going on!"

"Great idea, Cuz," Trap replied.

But even from the top of his shoulders, I couldn't see worth a crumb of cheese!

"Benjamin, CLIMB up on top of my shoulders!" I told my nephew.

"Sure, Uncle!" he replied, scurrying to the top.

"Can you see anything?" I asked.

"Yup!" Benjamin squeaked. "The robots are loading the emperor and his daughter into the Galactic Garbage Shooter!"

Slimy space Swiss! We had to act fast.

"Run, Trap!" I called down to my cousin. "We need to STOP those robots!"

Trap dashed through the crowd as Benjamin and I WOBBLED back and forth. Just as we were about to lose our fur by tumbling off Trap's shoulders, we reached the Galactic Garbage Shooter. The rebel robot leader was about to give the order to shoot!

"STOP!" I squeaked.

The robot leader turned to us in surprise.

"It's those funny aliens who arrived this morning!" he said. "Who are you and what are you doing here?"

"We are **spacemice**, and we came here to track down the source of all that junk floating in space," I replied.

"You're at the source," the robot leader said. "The junk comes from this garbage shooter, which the emperor of Sparklina invented. The Cleanix aliens throw away things constantly—including robots!— to make room for newer models. And they do it by shooting the trash into *space*.

It's the emperor's fault!

I worked for the emperor for months, but he threw me away just like everything else. He replaced me with a newer model with an UNDERWATER feature!"

"That's terrible," I said sympathetically.

"No, it's **ridiculous**!" the robot exclaimed. "There are no oceans, lakes, or rivers on Cleanix. So it's a **useless** feature! And I still work! It's been the same for all these robots, too."

He gestured toward the other rebel robots.

"It's true!" cried a robot made of **SPACESHIP** parts. "I was thrown away because my owner didn't like my **color** anymore!"

"And I was thrown away and replaced by a model with **six screens** instead of five!" another robot shouted.

"You're right to be angry, but maybe

I was thrown away because of my color!

97

there's another **SOLUTION** to the problem," I suggested gently. "Sending the emperor and his family into space won't **change** the way the other Cleanix aliens behave."

"Maybe not, but it doesn't matter now," the robot leader replied. "From now on, the **robots rule**! Begin the countdown!"

"Ready for **LAUNCH**," another robot announced. **"Ten . . . nine . . . eight . . . seven . . . six . . ."**

They didn't want me anymore!

WHAT A SURPRISE!

I covered my eyes with my **Paws** so I wouldn't have to see what happened to the emperor and his family.

"Wait!" someone cried. "*F2-C7*, is that really you? I can't believe it!"

It was ROBOTIX!

"F1-C7! What a surprise!" replied the robot leader.

Then he STOPPED the countdown.

I uncovered my eyes and saw the two robots hugging each other, *sparks* flying everywhere.

GREAT GALAXIES! They knew each other?!

"You're still **intact**," the robot leader said to Robotix in disbelief. "So you weren't

demolished after all?"

"No, I still carry out all my functions perfectly on the spaceship **MouseStar 1**," Robotix replied happily. "And, not to brag, but I'm much more advanced than their onboard computer."

"**Lucky you!**" the robot leader said, still in awe.

"And what are you doing these days?" Robotix asked.

"Well, I was working for the emperor's family, but after just six months of service, they substituted a **new** robot for me," F2-C7 explained. "On this planet, they throw everything away **CONSTANTLY**. That's why we robots have decided to **rebel**!"

"I see," Robotix said thoughtfully. "But maybe there's another solution . . ."

The two robots began to chatter in another **language**. Of course I didn't understand a thing!

"Um, excuse me, Robotix," I said politely. "Can you tell me what's going on?"

"Oh, I apologize, Captain Stiltonix," he replied. "I forgot to introduce you! The robot leader is my cousin F2-C7!"

"Y-your cousin?" I asked, stunned.

"Yes, my real name isn't Robotix—it's *F1-C7*," Robotix explained. "F2-C7 and I were built together in the same astroyear. But when I moved to the *MouseStar 1*, I lost track of him."

"And now here we are!" exclaimed the robot leader. "And my clever cousin has an interesting idea about how to SOLVE our problem."

"That's superstellar!" I exclaimed. "What's the plan?"

"Robotix suggested that we use the *MouseStar 1*'s garbage-recycling machine."

"Of course!" I squeaked. "The Stellar Garbage Sortrix would be perfect for the job!"

"We could bring the Sortrix here to Cleanix to RECYCLE the planet's garbage," Thea agreed. "That way all the trash will have a **new life**! And, of course, we'll encourage the Cleanix to throw out less."

"Well done, Robotix," I congratulated him. "That's a **GENIUS** idea!"

"Could you let us down now?" the emperor called anxiously.

"Yes," I agreed. "We wouldn't want someone to press the *launch* button by mistake!"

A New Era for Cleanix

The rebel robots released the emperor, his wife, and his daughter from the Galactic Garbage Shooter.

"Thank you for your help," Emperor Sparkle said. "Without the spacemice, who knows where we might have ended up."

"That's easy," Trap replied. "You'd be in space!"

Shimmer threw her arms around my cousin's neck.

"My hero!" she exclaimed. "You and your friends saved us."

"I'm very sorry for having doubted you," the emperor said to me. "When you went

My hero!

to the **DARK** side of the planet, I thought that you were our ENEMY . . ."

"I told you that the spacemice were our **friends**, dad!" Shimmer interjected.

"You're right," the emperor told his daughter. "I should have listened to you."

Then he turned to me.

"And I should have trusted you, Captain," he said. "Now what can I do to make up for it?"

"Solving your garbage problem would be a great start!" I replied.

"But that's why we invented the Galactic Garbage Shooter," he said.

"I'm afraid POLLUTING space with your junk isn't the answer," Thea said sternly. "You should try using things until they no longer work, instead of just throwing good things away. Then you can recycle any garbage that you accumulate."

"Recycle the garbage?" the emperor asked, a puzzled expression on his face. "Okay, but how?"

"The Stellar Garbage Sortrix, a machine we developed, can recycle ninety-nine point nine percent of all our garbage," Thea explained. "That way we don't throw anything away—not even cheese rinds!"

"We've already promised the robots we will lend you the Sortrix," I added. "That way you can clean up your planet from TOP to bottom. And you'll give new life to things that used to be garbage."

The emperor gave me a serious look. Black holey galaxies, I couldn't tell what he was thinking! But then he broke into a GRIN.

"Captain Stiltonix, I must admit that this is an **excellent** idea!" he exclaimed.

Then he turned to F2-C7.

"I'm sorry I tossed you out without thinking," he said contritely. "Since you

I'm sorry!

Let's start recycling!

know garbage so well, I would like to make you Cleanix's official *Recycling Manager*. What do you think?"

"I **accept** the position, Your Highness," F2-C7 replied enthusiastically. "Let's start recycling right away."

What a relief! We had come up with a solution for an incredibly **messy** problem. I activated my WRIST COMMUNICATOR and called the *MouseStar 1* to tell everyone on board the good news. Unfortunately for me, Sally answered!

"What's the word, *Captain*?" she asked eagerly.

"Umm . . . er . . . I — I . . ." I stuttered. *COSMIC CHEDDAR!*

My nerves always took

Captain Stiltonix?

109

over whenever I had a chance to talk to that fabumouse rodent!

"Captain Stiltonix?" Sally asked. "You're not coming in **CLEARLY**!"

Luckily, Trap came to my rescue.

"The captain's wrist communicator isn't working well," Trap explained. "He

wanted to ask you to prepare the Stellar Garbage Sortrix for transport to Cleanix. We're loaning it to the emperor so he and his people can clean up their planet."

Great job!

"Copy that!" Sally replied.

From that day on, the Cleanix aliens began an era of **respect** for their environment—and for their objects. Before we returned to *MouseStar 1*, the emperor threw a party in honor of the spacemice.

It was **superstellar**!

Finally, it was time for good-byes: Robotix and his cousin **F** **2** **-** **C** **7** promised they would meet again within two galactic years, and **SHIMMER** convinced Trap to return to Cleanix as soon as his new spacesuit got crumpled.

The Cleanix aliens insisted on giving us thank-you **GIFTS**. Mine was the highest **honor** in the city: A statue made from **RECYCLED** metal was installed on Sparklina's main street, right next to the one of former emperor Reginald Shiny!

MOUSY METEORITES, what an honor!

Our mission complete, we returned to *MouseStar 1*. Now space would be clean again, and I could get to work writing about our encounter with the **Cleanix aliens**. And, of course, I had to reschedule my *dinner date* with Sally! Though, first I'd have to find the **courage** to actually squeak with her, snout-to-snout. But that, dear rodent friends, is an intergalactic adventure for another day!

Don't miss any adventures of the Spacemice!

#1 Alien Escape

#2 You're Mine, Captain!

#3 Ice Planet Adventure

#4 The Galactic Goal

#5 Rescue Rebellion

#6 The Underwater Planet

#7 Beware! Space Junk!

Up Next!

#8 Away in a Star Sled

Be sure to read all my fabumouse adventures!

Geronimo Stilton

LOST TREASURE OF THE EMERALD EYE
#1 Lost Treasure of the Emerald Eye

THE CURSE OF THE CHEESE PYRAMID
#2 The Curse of the Cheese Pyramid

CAT AND MOUSE IN A HAUNTED HOUSE
#3 Cat and Mouse in a Haunted House

I'M TOO FOND OF MY FUR!
#4 I'm Too Fond of My Fur!

FOUR MICE DEEP IN THE JUNGLE
#5 Four Mice Deep in the Jungle

PAWS OFF, CHEDDARFACE!
#6 Paws Off, Cheddarface!

RED PIZZAS FOR A BLUE COUNT
#7 Red Pizzas for a Blue Count

ATTACK OF THE BANDIT CATS
#8 Attack of the Bandit Cats

A FABUMOUSE VACATION FOR GERONIMO
#9 A Fabumouse Vacation for Geronimo

ALL BECAUSE OF A CUP OF COFFEE
#10 All Because of a Cup of Coffee

IT'S HALLOWEEN, YOU 'FRAIDY MOUSE!
#11 It's Halloween, You 'Fraidy Mouse!

MERRY CHRISTMAS, GERONIMO!
#12 Merry Christmas, Geronimo!

THE PHANTOM OF THE SUBWAY
#13 The Phantom of the Subway

THE TEMPLE OF THE RUBY OF FIRE
#14 The Temple of the Ruby of Fire

THE MONA MOUSA CODE
#15 The Mona Mousa Code

A CHEESE-COLORED CAMPER
#16 A Cheese-Colored Camper

WATCH YOUR WHISKERS, STILTON!
#17 Watch Your Whiskers, Stilton!

SHIPWRECK ON THE PIRATE ISLANDS
#18 Shipwreck on the Pirate Islands

MY NAME IS STILTON, GERONIMO STILTON
#19 My Name Is Stilton, Geronimo Stilton

SURF'S UP, GERONIMO!
#20 Surf's Up, Geronimo!

#21 The Wild, Wild West

#22 The Secret of Cacklefur Castle

A Christmas Tale

#23 Valentine's Day Disaster

#24 Field Trip to Niagara Falls

#25 The Search for Sunken Treasure

#26 The Mummy with No Name

#27 The Christmas Toy Factory

#28 Wedding Crasher

#29 Down and Out Down Under

#30 The Mouse Island Marathon

#31 The Mysterious Cheese Thief

Christmas Catastrophe

#32 Valley of the Giant Skeletons

#33 Geronimo and the Gold Medal Mystery

#34 Geronimo Stilton, Secret Agent

#35 A Very Merry Christmas

#36 Geronimo's Valentine

#37 The Race Across America

#38 A Fabumouse School Adventure

#39 Singing Sensation

#40 The Karate Mouse

#41 Mighty Mount Kilimanjaro

#42 The Peculiar Pumpkin Thief

#43 I'm Not a Supermouse!

#44 The Giant Diamond Robbery

#45 Save the White Whale!

#46 The Haunted Castle

#47 Run for the Hills, Geronimo!

#48 The Mystery in Venice

#49 The Way of the Samurai

#50 This Hotel Is Haunted!

#51 The Enormouse Pearl Heist

#52 Mouse in Space!

#53 Rumble in the Jungle

#54 Get into Gear, Stilton!

#55 The Golden Statue Plot

#56 Flight of the Red Bandit

The Hunt for the Golden Book

#57 The Stinky Cheese Vacation

#58 The Super Chef Contest

#59 Welcome to Moldy Manor

The Hunt for the Curious Cheese

#60 The Treasure of Easter Island

#61 Mouse House Hunter

#62 Mouse Overboard!

The Hunt for the Secret Papyrus

#63 The Cheese Experiment

#64 Magical Mission

Join me and my friends as we travel through time in these very special editions!

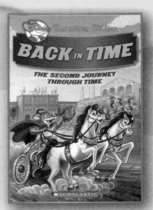

THE JOURNEY THROUGH TIME

BACK IN TIME:
THE SECOND JOURNEY THROUGH TIME

THE RACE AGAINST TIME
THE THIRD JOURNEY THROUGH TIME

Don't miss any of these exciting Thea Sisters adventures!

Thea Stilton and the Dragon's Code

Thea Stilton and the Mountain of Fire

Thea Stilton and the Ghost of the Shipwreck

Thea Stilton and the Secret City

Thea Stilton and the Mystery in Paris

Thea Stilton and the Cherry Blossom Adventure

Thea Stilton and the Star Castaways

Thea Stilton: Big Trouble in the Big Apple

Thea Stilton and the Ice Treasure

Thea Stilton and the Secret of the Old Castle

Thea Stilton and the Blue Scarab Hunt

Thea Stilton and the Prince's Emerald

Thea Stilton and the Mystery on the Orient Express

Thea Stilton and the Dancing Shadows

Thea Stilton and the Legend of the Fire Flowers

Thea Stilton and the Spanish Dance Mission

Thea Stilton and the Journey to the Lion's Den

Thea Stilton and the Great Tulip Heist

Thea Stilton and the Chocolate Sabotage

Thea Stilton and the Missing Myth

Thea Stilton and the Lost Letters

Thea Stilton and the Tropical Treasure

Thea Stilton and the Hollywood Hoax

Meet
GERONIMO STILTONOOT

He is a cavemouse — Geronimo Stilton's ancient ancestor! He runs the stone newspaper in the prehistoric village of Old Mouse City. From dealing with dinosaurs to dodging meteorites, his life in the Stone Age is full of adventure!

#1 The Stone of Fire

#2 Watch Your Tail!

#3 Help, I'm in Hot Lava!

#4 The Fast and the Frozen

#5 The Great Mouse Race

#6 Don't Wake the Dinosaur!

#7 I'm a Scaredy-Mouse!

#8 Surfing for Secrets

#9 Get the Scoop, Geronimo!

#10 My Autosaurus Will Win!

#11 Sea Monster Surprise

#12 Paws Off the Pearl!

Don't miss any of my magical special edition adventures!

THE KINGDOM OF FANTASY

THE QUEST FOR PARADISE:
THE RETURN TO THE KINGDOM OF FANTASY

THE AMAZING VOYAGE:
THE THIRD ADVENTURE IN THE KINGDOM OF FANTASY

THE DRAGON PROPHECY:
THE FOURTH ADVENTURE IN THE KINGDOM OF FANTASY

THE VOLCANO OF FIRE:
THE FIFTH ADVENTURE IN THE KINGDOM OF FANTASY

THE SEARCH FOR TREASURE:
THE SIXTH ADVENTURE IN THE KINGDOM OF FANTASY

THE ENCHANTED CHARMS:
THE SEVENTH ADVENTURE IN THE KINGDOM OF FANTASY

THE PHOENIX OF DESTINY:
AN EPIC KINGDOM OF FANTASY ADVENTURE

THE HOUR OF MAGIC:
THE EIGHTH ADVENTURE IN THE KINGDOM OF FANTASY

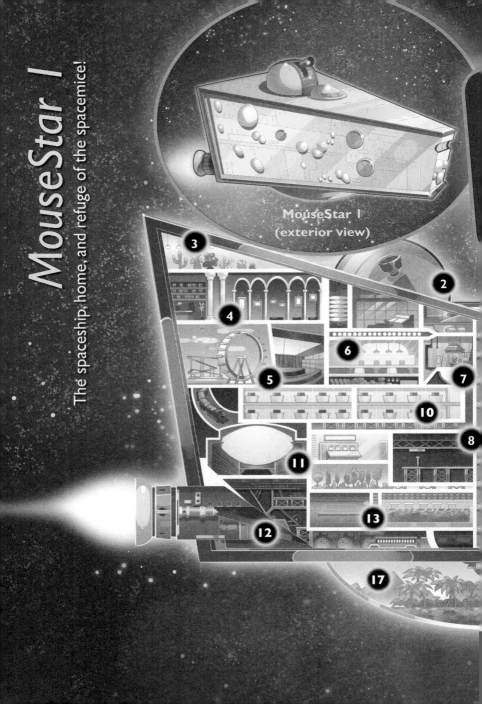

MouseStar 1

The spaceship, home, and refuge of the spacemice!

MouseStar 1
(exterior view)

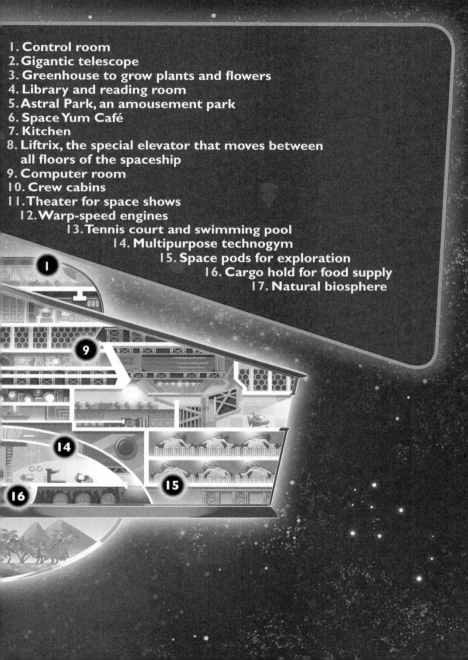

1. Control room
2. Gigantic telescope
3. Greenhouse to grow plants and flowers
4. Library and reading room
5. Astral Park, an amousement park
6. Space Yum Café
7. Kitchen
8. Liftrix, the special elevator that moves between all floors of the spaceship
9. Computer room
10. Crew cabins
11. Theater for space shows
12. Warp-speed engines
13. Tennis court and swimming pool
14. Multipurpose technogym
15. Space pods for exploration
16. Cargo hold for food supply
17. Natural biosphere

Dear mouse friends,
thanks for reading,
and good-bye until the next book.
See you in outer space!